Arthur Sketchley

Mrs. Brown's Christmas Box

Arthur Sketchley

Mrs. Brown's Christmas Box

ISBN/EAN: 9783337382698

Printed in Europe, USA, Canada, Australia, Japan

Cover: Foto ©Andreas Hilbeck / pixelio.de

More available books at **www.hansebooks.com**

Mrs. Brown's Christmas Box.

BY

ARTHUR SKETCHLEY,

AUTHOR OF "MRS. BROWN IN THE HIGHLANDS," "THE BROWN PAPERS,"
ETC. ETC.

LONDON:

GEORGE ROUTLEDGE AND SONS,
THE BROADWAY, LUDGATE.

INTRODUCTORY REMARKS.

Lor bless you, tell you about Christmas! I should think I could indeed, as in course I remembers werry well lots of Christmases, and all about 'em as parties as talks of bein' merry; but only 'em can call 'em so as 'ave lived a short time in this 'ere world of sorrers and wexations, for I'm sure I remembers as 'eavy sorrers 'ave come at Christmas-time, as makes 'em seem more sorrerful, and I've know'd many as 'ave said as they 'ated the name of Christmas, thro' troubles 'appenin' to come jest then.

But, lor bless you! it ain't no use a-givin' in to them thoughts, for the world will go on jest the same, Christmas or no Christmas, as comes but once a year, and we must take it as it comes.

Some says as they likes a old-fashioned Christmas, with everythink a-freezin' like mad, as is all werry well for them as 'ave plenty to eat and drink, with lots of coals and blankets, tho' certingly them werry mild Christmases makes parties

1

forget the poor, no doubt, and must be ruination to the butcher's meat, let alone the poulterer.

And no doubt cold is more 'ealthy, for as the sayin' is, a green yule, as is French for Christmas, makes a fat churchyard ; but I think them sayin's was all werry well when there was plenty to eat and drink, and not when meat's a shillin' a pound, and obligated for to be brought over from Australier, as no doubt may be nurishin' tho' not nice, and no wonder as parties would rather go over there and eat it, than 'ave it brought to them, as a sea woyage can't be good for the same, as I've 'eard say as it is for Dublin stout and sherry wine, as is made dearer and ain't worth drinkin' afore it's been at sea.

It's wonderful what the sea will do, for I've knowed it myself bring many a boy to 'is senses with one woyage, like young Camplin, and certingly is a fine thing for the 'ealth, partikler anythink bein' wrong in the chest, tho' some do say as it 'ave encouraged many parties for to rob the till, thro' a-lookin' out for to escape by sea, as a many 'as done, tho' some caught in the hact, the same as that 'ere German as killed the old gent in the railway, and was knabbed in landin', as I've seen the werry spot in the ocean as they took 'im on myself, as is close ag'in Merryka.

And certingly if it 'adn't been for a sea woyage as Em'ly Crattle went thro', she'd never 'ave been Tom Markham's wife, as was a-courtin' long afore he went to New Zealand, as I never could make out what he could see in 'er for to shed tears over in partin', and thinks to myself, my lady, you'll never see 'im no more, for she was no beauty, and a whiny temper.

But, law bless you, she was sharp enough, for if she didn't go arter 'im by the next ship and got there the werry day afore he was a-goin' to marry a werry nice young gal as he'd met aboard the same ship as he went out in, as led to words thro' her two brothers bein' of the Hirish persuasion, but Em'ly stuck to 'im and he 'ad to marry 'er, as were as well, poor thing, for she didn't trouble 'im long thro' bein' took by the savages, as they do say eat 'er, not as ever I will believe as they can be such beasts as that, any'ow she were never 'card on more, as is over twenty year ago, and he's been married ag'in jest on nineteen, for 'is eldest come over and called in to see me as is turned eighteen, as shows 'ow time passes all the same, wherever you go, or whatever you do.

Poor old Mrs. Crattle, she never was the same woman ag'in arter Em'ly left, not but what they quarreled like cats and dogs, as the sayin' is, while they was together, for I never shall forget the last Christmas they was together, as Mrs. Crattle 'ad put in for a Christmas club, as brought 'er a goose and a bottle of gin, and nothink wouldn't do but I must go and 'elp eat it, as is a thing as it don't do to dine off entire in my opinion, and is too much for supper.

Tho' I 'ave knowed parties give it for a weddin', the same as them Jemisons as lived close ag'in Lim'us Church, thro' 'im bein' churchwarden, and not credit for a bundle of wood, and set in the green-baise pew of a Sunday, as proud as Lucifers, as the sayin' 'is, an' 'is wife, all dressed in silk and feathers, as were a reg'lar match maker, and so got young Flunker to marry 'er eldest but four, as well she might, for there was nine on 'em, as plain as pike-staffs, as the sayin' is, and 'im nothink but a clerk, as lost 'is place, thro' losin' of some money, as he said were cut out of 'is pocket a-goin' to the bank without a chain round 'is waist, yet proud to the last.

Young Flunker he wasn't nothink partikler, thro' 'is father bein' in the boot and shoe line, as was all brought from the country ready made, and 'owever they could write over 'em in the winders,

"Our own make," I can't think, but that's their business.

Woll, that night as I went to eat Mrs. Crattle's goose, was the night afore Sarah Jemison's weddin', as lived jest round the corner, and Mrs. Crattle she'd been in a-lendin' a 'elpin' 'and, for that Mrs. Jemison were a born fool, and 'ad brought them gals up reg'lar useless dawdles.

Of all the 'ouses as ever I did go into it were that Jemison's as pig-styes is a pallis to, for Mrs. Crattle she come 'ome jest as I got there, and asked me if I'd mind jest a-showin' them gals 'ow to get up their clear muslings, as 'ad been that blue-bagged as I says must be passed thro' cold water afore bein' ironed.

Well, Em'ly come in arterwards, a-sayin' she'd put down the goose; well, and what with doin' one thing and the other, it was over nine when we got 'ome to Mrs. Crattle's, and no sooner opened the door, thro' Em'ly 'avin' the key, than we was nearly knocked back'ards with the smell of coals in the drippin' pan; I says to Mrs. Crattle, "Mussy on us, that goose is a-burnin'."

We all 'urries down into the kitehen, and there was a sight, that gal fast asleep afore the fire, with the goose a-standin' still, burnt as black as coal, and the drippin' pan in flames.

Mrs. Crattle gave a scream as woke up that gal as tried to stand us out as she 'adn't never been asleep, and then Mrs. Crattle and Em'ly got to them 'igh words over that goose thro' 'er 'avin' left it and come into Jemison's when 'er mother 'ad begged and prayed 'er to mind it, as in course was foolishness to leave it to a child like that Sarah Saunders, as was only jest turned eleven, as Em'ly were that wild with, and a-goin' to give 'er a box on the ear, missed 'er, 'avin' knocked over the bottle of gin as were standin' on the dresser, as made that gal run out a-'ollerin' murder, as brought a crowd round the 'ouse, so I were glad to slip away in the confusion, glad to get out of the row, a-knowin' as Brown would storm if he 'eard about it, as in a gin'ral way don't care much about Christmas.

I ain't no partikler reason to care about it myself, for I'm sure what with cleanin' up for it, with the sweeps, and a-slavin' and drivin' to get ready ; and then a Christmas party, with a reg'lar row, as in general turns out, tho' I never 'ad but once, thro' a-tryin' to bring all the family together, as Brown set 'is face ag'in from the fust, a-sayin' as they'd be sure to fall out, as proved true.

I says, " And more shame for 'em, as did ought to be thankful for a good dinner, and try to forget all them hanermosities as will rankle in the 'art with some, and is apt to break out over a full stomich, and · pre'aps thro' takin' a little more than usual in the sperritual line.

Well, we 'ad the party, and of all the rows as ever I 'eard it was that Christmas-day, and all thro' a word, as were meant in jest, as the sayin' is, but certingly did jest put all the party out, for Brown never meant nothink when he said, jokin'-like, arter dinner, "As now the beasts was fed they'd be quiet," as made old Mrs. Barnes, as were a-noddin', bust into tears, and 'er son, as is our Jane's 'usban', took it up 'ot, a-sayin', "As no man livin' should call 'is mother a beast, not sleepin' or wakin', neither," as busted out of the room all in a flurry like, and went upstairs and flopped 'erself on to my bed, and as nigh as a toucher overlaid Jane's babby as were a-sleepin' there.

Jane, she certingly did forget 'erself in callin' of 'er 'usban's mother a slaughterin' old bullock, as she couldn't never abear afore that, as I were not aware on, or never would 'ave inwited the old lady along with 'em, as never were a friend of mine, and things might 'ave sobered down, only as bad luck would 'ave it, Jane give old Mrs. Barnes a shove, as slipped off the bed and put 'er elber out,

as said Jane 'ad murdered 'er, and brought up
Barnes with 'er screams, as flew out at 'is wife and
mother both, a-sayin' they was the cuss of 'is life
on the staircase, and up comes Brown and says
he wouldn't 'ave 'is place turned into a bear-garding
for nobody, as put old Mrs. Barnes in that rage
as certingly were a-showin' 'er legs disgraceful,
a-strugglin' on the floor, not as Brown illuded to
'em; and jest as we was a-quietin' down, the kittle
biled over into the kitchen fire, and scalded the gal's
foot, and made that 'orrible tench thro' the 'ouse
as made Barnes say he'd as soon set in the dust-
'ole, as I couldn't stand sich impidence, and told
'im plain to 'is face, as a dung'ill were about 'is
size, thro' bein' a rank coward, for I know'd as
he'd threatened to strike my gal ag'in and ag'in.

But, law! I'd better 'ave let it alone, for in course
she took 'is part, and off they all went 'ome afore
tea, old 'ooman and all, as were just as well, for
Brown's married sister and 'er 'usban' come in
soon arter, as is own uncle to Barnes, as married
our Jane, as would 'ave quarreled, as sure as eggs
is eggs, as the sayin' is.

I was reg'lar put out, and thro' never being
friends with Brown's sister, as spilte 'er boy Alfred
that dreadful as 'ad come to see me three days

afore Christmas, and for to keep 'im out of mischief I'd give 'im some receipts, as I'd got in a book, to copy out for Mrs. Camplin, and werry nigh brought on words atween us for life, as I sent 'em over to 'er all of a hurry, thro' knowin' she was all behind with 'er Christmas, as come in the next day, and says, " Mrs. Brown, next time as you wants to play off your jokes, don't try me, as don't like it."

I says, " Whatever do you mean by jokes ? as ain't got such a thing about me."

She says, " Please to read this," and 'ands me that paper as Alfred 'ad copied out for 'er, and I thought I should 'ave dropped, for he'd been and wrote :—

Receipt for Jelly.

Fust soak your feet well, as is sure to require it, then serape and pare 'em, put 'em in loo warm water, and keep 'em there till they simmers, and the flesh comes away easy from the bone, then strain 'em off, and put 'em in a clean pan to eool. Pass 'em thro' jelly bag, flavour and sweeten 'em to taste, and serve up in shape or glasses. N.B. Pigs' feet will do as well for the purpose, if you ain't got no others 'andy.

Jugged 'Air.

Let your 'air 'ang 'ead downwards long enough,

then draw and cut it, put it in a jar, bake in a slow oven, with gravy beef, and season to taste.

'Ow to Dress your 'Air.

When it's been 'anging long enough, wash it well in salt and water, stuff it full of crumbs of bread and sweet 'erbs, and suet chopped fine, rub it well with salt butter, let it be three-quarters 'of a 'our before a brisk fire, without a-burnin', then dress it up 'ot with current jelly and gravy.

'Ow to Cure your 'Ams.

Pickle 'em well in strong brine, rub in salt peter freely, put 'em up the chimbly to dry, keep 'em there as long as you likes. They may require soakin' before usin'

'Ow to Dry your Cheeks.

Mind as your cheeks is young and tender, the plumper the better. Scrape 'em well if 'airy. Singe the 'air well out of your ears, rub in salt daily, keep 'em in pickle till they're fully swelled, let the brine flow over freely, then dry 'em up the chimbly till you wants to use 'em.

I says, " Well, mum, the receipts is good enough, but no doubt that boy 'ave been a-playin' the fool, as seemed to pacify 'er, not as I could see what she 'ad to growl about, as could see what was meant.

I didn't say nothink about the trick as that boy 'ad played me, and shouldn't if 'is mother arter supper 'adn't begun a-blowin' about 'is larnin', a-sayin' he'd be a Wice-Chancelor.

I says, "I'll back 'im for the Wice any 'ow, but don't seem to see no chance of anythink else."

Well them words put 'er back up, and she went on so that I got reg'lar aggrawated, and went and fetched that rubbish as he'd wrote, and if 'er and Barnes and Brown didn't set to a-larfin' theirselves pretty nigh to death over it.

"Well," I says, "it may be werry clever, but I don't see it," and was a-goin' to be cross over it; but when they come to read 'em over to me ag'in, I couldn't 'elp a-smilin' myself, as didn't want things to go unpleasant, so we all shook 'ands and 'ad a friendly glass; but when they was gone I agreed along with Brown as it were runnin' risks 'avin' them family parties, and am thankful as the others went away afore the Barnes' come, as them two brothers never can't agree; not but what there's some as meets and parts friendly and plea-sant at Christmas, the same as some 'ave troubles and some 'ave sorrers, so, as I said afore, we must take it as it comes, the rough with the smooth, and make the best on it. Whether it's Christmas or any other time as will come round, whether we likes it or lumps it, as the sayin' is.

Not as I shall ever forget old Mrs. McCulloch, as 'ad a son in India as sent 'er over silk shawls, omangoes, and Chutnee, with ginger and chess men, and fans and feathers, with a tiger's skin, and elephant's teeth, and if she could 'ave eat gold might 'ave 'ad it, thro' 'im 'avin' made nineteen woyages, as was all little fortins to 'im, and come 'ome as reg'lar as clock-work every year, jest as the green peas was in season.

Well, when I lived out Stepney way, she lived oppersit as was 'igher rented 'ouses and run to over forty-five, rent and taxes, with a nice garding back and front.

Well, it was one Christmas-evo as I were a-takin' in from the baker-boy a cake as I'd made and sent to tho hoven, tho' never trusted my mince-pies out of my sight, when I see the postman come out of Mrs. McCulloch's gate, and was a-tellin' that boy as the cake were burnt shameful, as must 'ave been too quick a oven, when I see the old lady's servint a-shettin' all the shetters in a wiolent 'urry, as give me quite a turn, a-thinkin' as pre'aps the old lady might 'ave been took sudden 'erself, as were that lusty with a 'ot supper every night, and brandy in 'er gruel, as the steam on took away your breath.

So I give the cake to Mrs. Challin, as were 'elpin' me 'arf a day, and only slipped on a shawl, and over I goes to see what were up.

As soon as I got to the door I 'eard 'er a-goin' on frightful in the parlour, and when the woman opened the door, she says, "Come in, Mrs. Brown, and do 'elp me for to comfort my poor dear missus, as is 'art-broken thro' er trouble."

I says, "Whatever is the matter?"

She says, "Oh, he's gone, 'er only son."

I was shocked dreadful, and goes into the parlour, and there set the old lady a-giviu' tung awful.

So I says, "Come, come, Mrs. McCulloch, you mustn't take on like this."

But she wouldn't 'ear nothink, but as luck would 'ave it, who should knock at the door but Father McCleary, as is 'er own sister's son, thro' all bein' of the Hirish persuasion.

We told 'im what were amiss, as soon made 'is aunt shet up 'er 'owls, and then says, "Where's the letter?" as were a-layin' on the ground, as he no sooner set eyes on than he said, "He's no more dead than I am; it's all a mistake."

Says Mrs. McCulloch, "Sure, now, you're deceivin' me, Mick, I know he's dead, for didn't I 'ear the death-watch and dog a-'owlin' myself last night."

He turned on 'er quite sharp, and told 'er not to talk no such nonsense as that, but to listen, and sure enough it was all a mistake, for the letter wasn't for 'er at all, but for a good old widder in the same name, as 'ad got a pension thro' er 'usban's death, as 'ad been dead over a year in the name of Patrick McCulloch.

Certingly the letter would 'ave give anyone a turn, thro' a-beginnin' by a-sayin', "In consequence of the death of Patrick McCulloch," as Patrick was 'er boy's name, but worth ten thousand dead-'uns, and come 'ome the next spring more lively than ever.

But the shock spilte the old lady's Christmas, and made 'er that ill as Father McCleary told me 'isself as he didn't think she'd get over it; but, law! she did, and lived over seven year arter that, and see 'er son retire from the sea, and settle down with a wife and two children within two doors off 'er, as were a comfort to 'er, no doubt, afore she died, tho' she told me 'erself as she couldn't abear a bone in 'er daughter-in-law's body, and didn't think as she'd ever rear either of them children, as she mismanaged fearful, as both lived in spite of 'er, tho' three as were born arter never did thrive, and they berried two on 'em afore they left Stepney, and so it is as the world goes on.

But, law! I could tell you enough about Christmas for to fill a book with, as some might like to read, as is the way to learn, we all knows, but did ought to be read careful like, and not in a 'urry, like old Mrs. McCulloch's letter; not as ever she read one in a 'urry ag'in, for the werry sight of one throwed 'er into that fright as she always sent for Father McCleary to read it to 'er, so it's lucky as she did get but two a year, or all 'is time would 'ave been took up readin' 'er letters, as 'ad enough to do, partikler about Christmas time, but always werry lively, and would look in and eat a bit of cold puddin' and a glass of my ginger cordial, as warmed 'im up, as is what I should wish to do by every one, as I 'artily wishes

"A Merry Christmas and 'Appy New Year,
A pocket full of money, and a cellar full of beer,"

as the sayin' did used to be.

CONTENTS.

MRS. BROWN'S CHRISTMAS-BOX.

I.

MRS. BROWN AND THE WAITS.

I'M sure I'm one as loves music as well as anybody in its place, and 'ave give many a penny to them orgins, and never did say nothink as were 'arsh-like escept to them boy German bands, as did used to kick up a awful ullerbeloo that time as Mrs. Padwick's niece 'ad the hairy sepelas in 'er 'ead, as I do think were brought on by usin' of them 'air-dyes as she tied 'er 'ead up in with 'ot cabbage-leaves every night a-goin' to bed, and got up with 'er 'ead all swelled up like a bushel-measure with a breakin' out all down 'er face like small-pox come out favourable, and the fever runnin' that 'igh as were delirious two nights runnin', as I set up with 'er myself.

Well, it was when she were at the werry wust as that boy band come round one mornin' and made that beastly noise under the winder, and wouldn't go away, as I throwed water over 'em and then

called the perlice as soon started em off abusin' me
frightful in their gibberish.

I always did used to like to 'ear the Waits at
Christmas-time till that Christmas as Liza Somers
died as I nussed long afore I were married thro' a
decline, and went off like a lamb, poor dear, at the
last, and then arter that I couldn't abear the sound
on 'em for many years, but 'ad got over it like till
about three Christmases ago, when they seemed to
aggrawate me beyond bearin', and some'ow they
was more louder than ever, and more on 'em, as
seemed to be a-breakin' out fresh all night long all
down our street.

Whether it were as I ain't as good a sleeper as
I did used to be, or am a-gettin' fidgety in my old
age, as Brown says, I don't know ; but of all the
aggrawatin' things as ever did torment me it was
them Waits, as would play me up, back and front,
every night, till I couldn't abear it no longer.

I think, pre'aps, as solemn music in the night
is a thing for to make any one think as ain't asleep,
as did used to seem to soothe poor Liza Somers,
as would lay a-listenin' to it with 'er 'ands clasped
by the 'our together, as couldn't sleep for 'er cough,
and would sometimes sing 'erself to sleep, poor
dear, thro' 'avin' been a sweet singer when in 'ealth,
and would bring the tears in your eyes with
" Halice Grey " and " Daily the Trubydoor," as

she sung lovely, and were offered 'undreds to go
on the stage; so she liked the Waits when played
solemn, as any one might, but not "Up in a
Balloon, Boys," and "Champagne Charlie," along
wi' a lot of walzes and rubbish as ain't pleasant
when you're jest a-droppin' off.

So I says to Brown one night, "Drat them
Waits," as woke 'im up with a blast, as only
says, "All right," and were off ag'in, as I do
believe would sleep sound over a powder-mill
blowin' up with a 'undred thousand trumpets a-
blowin' up too in 'is ear all the time, as 'is own
snores sounds like the echoes on, with a 'arty
supper of black puddin' layin' on 'is back.

It were jest the week afore Christmas as one
bitter night they seemed to come down our street,
them musicianers, wuss than ever, and the music were
that aggrawatin' as I'd gone to bed in good time
thro' a cold, and wanted for to sleep, but couldn't
for them Waits, and why ever they're called so I
can't make out, as no doubt means wakes, as is
what they really are.

If it 'adn't been so cold, I do think as I should
'ave took and shied water over 'em, tho' it wouldn't
'ave done no good, for I weren't by no means sure
as they was nigh enough to ketch it, besides I
didn't care about a-openin' of the winder, as might
give me a chill, so there I was a-loyin' and a-

listenin' till I 'eard 'em a-dyin' away down the
street with "Let me kiss 'im for 'is mother." As
I says to myself you may in welcome, if you'll let
me go to sleep.

I 'adn't 'ardly dropped off when a-rattlin' polker
or a somethink like that as were bein' played, jest
under our winder, on the 'ornet, woke me up ag'in;
I never 'eard anythink like that 'ornet, as seemed
to go right thro' my 'ead, with the clock only
strikin' twelve, and might go on till two or three, I
knowed; so I gets out of bed, and goes to the
winder, and if them fellers wasn't in our front
garding, one with a short 'ornet to 'is mouth, a-
blowin' like mad, and the other with a long
one as he pushed in and out, for all the world like
blowin' thro' a telescope, as jest then stopped for to
take their breath.

So I knocks at the winder and says, "Go away,
do, with your noise, a-distractin' of people out of
their beds at this time of night."

But, law! they didn't take no notice, thro' not a-
'earin' me, as must 'ave distracted their 'earin'
with their noise, I should say.

So I opens the winder a little bit, with a thick
shawl round my 'ead, and says, "Do be off with
you, or I'll make my good gentleman get up to
you."

One on 'em looks up, a-touchin' of 'is 'at quite

respectful-like, sayin', "Is there any partikler tune, mum, as we could 'ave the pleasure of lullin' you off with ?"

I says, "I don't want no lullin', my good man, as could sleep sound but for your row, as nobody can't want this time of night, I'm sure."

He says, " I'm sure it's not for pleasure we does it such a bitter cold night as this, as we've been at it ever since eleven this mornin'."

I says, " You must be fond of music."

" Fond of music !" he says, "why it's starvin' work bein' out such a night as this."

" Well, then," I says, " if you feels it so, why not go 'ome to your own beds, and let other people get their rest ?"

He says, " We're tryin' to earn a penny, and ain't 'ad no luck to-night."

" Well," I says, " I don't mind a-givin' you a trifle if you'll go," and shots down the winder thro' feelin' chilly, that sharp as the pulley rope give way, for I 'eard it fall with a lump inside, and knowed as I couldn't get it up no more. So 'avin' got tuppence as I meant to give 'em, I puts in a bit of paper and goes into the next room to ourn, as is a winder jest over the street-door, and opens it all of a 'urry for fear of takin' cold, and goes to jerk the tuppence out, when if I didn't give that flower-pot a shove as were a-standin' there on the sill, and out I pushed it, as did ought to 'ave been took in thro' bein' dead, and nothink only dreadful eye-sore.

I thought I should 'ave dropped, for my 'art misgive me, as it must 'ave fell on them men, for I didn't 'ear no crash of it a-breakin' on the step, nor yet no sound at all, tho' I was sure as it 'ad fell down flop.

Well, jest then I 'eard a noise with them two men down below, for I knowed as one on 'em 'ad come on to the door-step, and was a-lookin' up at me for to ketch what I'd promised 'em when I shet the winder down; so I pulls aside the blind, and see one on 'em a-settin' on the step a-restin' 'is 'ead on 'is 'and, and the other a-leanin' over 'im, as if in pain, and could 'ear 'im a-groanin'

I says, " Mussy on us, why surely I ain't never been and knocked that great 'eavy thing on to the poor man's 'ead," as I'd told that gal to take in over and over ag'in.

So I puts on my flannin gown, as well as my thick shawl, and down I goes to the street-door and listens.

I 'eard one say, "Does it 'urt you so dreadful bad."

" Yes," says the other, " that spiteful old devil 'ave been and stove in my eye."

I opens the door in a jiffey, and says, " Whatever is the matter?"

Says the man with the long 'ornet, " Why, an
old 'ooman on your fust floor 'ave been and throwed
a 'eavy flower-pot on this poor man's 'ead, as
were only tryin' to get a bit of bread for his wife
and children this bitter cold night."

I thought I should 'ave died, and says, " Stop
a-bit, my good man," and shets the door, and
down I goes and opens the kitchen-door, and
says, " come in 'ere, and let me see what's the
matter."

They both come in, one a-leadin' the other with
a frightful blow jest under 'is eye, a-lookin' like
death for paleness.

I see he were 'urt bad, so give 'im a little
drop of brandy, and never was more frightened
in my life, for I'd see that ere flower-pot a-layin'
all fragments on the door-step, as were a 'eavy one.

The fire weren't dead out, and the gal 'ad left a
bundle of wood there a-dryin' to light it in the
mornin', so I puts some sticks in with a bit of coal,
and says, " My good man, come and set near it and
warm yourself, for I'm sure I never meant to 'urt
you," and goes to my cupboard down there, where I
keeps a lot of things, and I werry soon made 'im a
plaster with a bit of lard, as I knowed would be
that coolin', and says, " the water 'll be 'ot iu a
minnit, and I'll give you a glass of somethink afore
you turns out, as did not go to do it, I do assure you."

Says the man as I'd been and 'urt, " No more
drink, I thank you, as will try to get 'ome."

" Well," I says, " Pre'aps you'd better, for your
cough seems werry bad."

" Yes," says the other man, " it always is on a
empty stomich, and he ain't 'ad nothink since a bit
of bread and cheese yesterday."

I says, " 'Ow's that? Why, I should 'ave
thought as you got lots to eat and drink where
you plays."

" Oh," he says, " we can get drink enough to
swim in, but no wittles."

" Well," I says, " will you 'ave a bit to eat 'ere,
or take it 'ome?"

They both said as they'd take it 'ome, so I puts
'em up some cold meat and bread and cheese in a
bit of newspaper, and give 'em a shillin', besides
the tuppences as they owned to 'avin' picked up,
and off they went a-leavin' of their address, as
were Lock's Fields, out Walworth way, and thankful I were to see 'em go, for at fust I were afraid as
the flower-pot 'ad proved fatal, as the sayin' is.

I couldn't get up next mornin' thro' my cold
bein' that bad, as no doubt that open winder 'adn't
done it no good.

Brown, as brought me up a cup of tea,
says, when I told 'im all about it, " If you goes
a-larkin' about at night with them Waits, you must

espect a cold;" and certingly I were as 'oarse as
ever a-ravin' could make me, tho' I never spoke
above my woice.

I were obligated for to keep the 'ouse for a
couple of days arter; but then thro' the weather
a-turnin' mild, I thought as I'd wenter as far as
Lock's Fields, thro' feelin' in a fidget about that
man.

It never were a part as I cared for, that Lock's
Fields, tho' I knowed Mrs. Child's as went out a-
nussin', as lived there, with a nice bit of garding,
when they was fields, as is all built over now, tho'
always too many open ditches for me.

It's over twenty years ago since I knowed the
part, as ain't got no better, and looks werry dickey,
as the sayin' is; and arter a deal of bother I
found out that 'ornet man's 'ouse, leastways 'is
lodgin's.

A werry wretched-lookin' woman, with a babby
in 'er arms, opened the door, as said as she were
Mrs. Fletcher, as were that 'ornet's name, as she
said were at 'ome in bed thro 'is cough bein' that
bad.

"Well," I says "I only called for to ask arter
'im thro' 'avin' caused 'im a accident with a flower-
pot on 'is 'ead."

"Oh," she says, " that wasn't much, and you
was that kind over it, as he told me, that he didn't

mind, and I'm sure would be glad to see you if you wouldn't mind a-steppin' in, tho' a poor place to ask you into, Mrs. Brown."

I says, "'Owever do you know my name?"

She says, "You've forgotten me, no doubt, but I remembers you werry well, when I lived with my aunt, Mrs. Charters, in the straw-bonnet line, near Poplar Church."

"What," I says, "are you Maria Bennet?"

She says, "In course I am, as went to live at Portsmouth, where my aunt died, as you remembers well."

I says, "I should think I did, indeed, as were a kind friend to me, as I'm sure I'd help any one as belonged to 'er," though I must say as I remembered as that gal had been a deal of trouble to 'er aunt, and spilte a Dunstable of mine in turnin' it.

She says, "Ah! I lost my best friend when I lost 'er, not as I've got any complaint ag'in my 'usban', as 'ave been a good 'usban' to me."

I says, "I'm glad to 'ear it," a-wonderin' in myself 'owever she could 'ave brought 'erself to marry a Wait.

She says, "Pray step in, Mrs. Brown, tho' I must say as I never espected you to find me poor like this.'

"Law," I says, "my good soul, I've been poor myself, and not ashamed to own it," and walks into

the parlour, as 'ad a bed in it, and there were that
poor man a-layin' down, tho' partly dressed.

He looked werry thin, and a deal wuss than by
candle light, but seemed glad to see me, tho' a
black eye as the flower-pot 'ad give 'im.

He said as he felt better, and 'oped to get out
along with 'is mate that evenin', as were a-goin' to
call for 'im.

So I says, "You ain't fit to go a-stayin' out
in the damp and cold with no mates nor Waits
neither; for," I says, "it's a constant drizzle, tho'
much milder, as feels as I may speak, thro' bein'
a old friend of your wife."

"Ah!" he says, "indeed; but," he says, "I
mustn't mind the weather, and don't believe as it
makes much difference to me, for my cough is that
bad summer and winter."

"But," I says, "it stands to reason as standin'
about at night a-blowin' away at that thing can't
do your cough no good."

He says, "Needs must when a certing person
drives."

"Ah!" I says, "that's as the sayin' is, but," I
says, "'ome's the place for you."

His wife she says, "We shan't have a 'ome
much longer if he can't get about, for we're
dreadful behind 'and in our rent now."

I says, "'Ow many children 'ave you got?"

She says, " Only this one left," and busts out a-cryin'.

He says to 'er, " Come, mother, 'old up," tho' I could see as 'is eyes were a-overflowin'

I says, " Let 'er be, as a good cry will do 'er good," for sorrers must 'ave their went the same as beer.

"Yes," she says, " and I do hope you'll escuse me, Mr. Brown, but I can't forget 'em," and sobbed fit to break 'er 'art, and then seemed better like, and told me all 'er troubles, tho' he tried to stop 'er.

I says to 'im, " Let 'er talk, as will do 'er good, and so it did, for she was a deal better when she told me all about it."

Poor soul, it were a 'ard trial for to berry two in measles within a fortnight, as 'ad pretty nigh beggared theirselves to lay 'em in the grave decent, and 'ad been in business for 'erself as a dressmaker at Portsmouth, and 'ad married 'im thro' bein' a sailor, as 'ad never been brought up to the music, tho' he'd learned the 'ornet when a boy, thro' 'is father bein' a maker of them instruments near Long Acre.

I set there ever so long a-talkin', and give 'er a trifle at partin', and a-tellin' 'er to let me know afore Christmas 'ow he were, thro' a-knowin' as Lady Wittles would stand their friend, if a good character, as I believed he were.

It were two days afore Christmas-eve, when up to my eyes in cleanin', leastways, a-lookin' arter them as was, when that poor woman come and told me as he were a deal wuss.

"Ah," I says, "went out, and got fresh cold, no doubt."

She says, "He did go out the other evenin' arter you was gone, but couldn't stop thro' a pain in 'is side, as pretty near bent 'im double, and I went for the doctor, as put 'im on a blister, and says he wants keepin' up."

I says, "I'll come and see 'im to-morrer, and you stop and 'ave a cup of tea," for the gal and Mrs. Challin 'ad just done theirn, and I were jest a-goin' to 'ave mine.

She says, "No, thank you, I rather get back, as 'ave left my little boy along with the landlady's gal, as is takin' care of 'im for me, thro' my 'usban's 'ead bein' that bad as he can't bear the least noise."

So in course I didn't press 'er, but let 'er 'ave a shillin' or two, and off she went that thankful as never were.

I was a-goin' to see Lady Wittles that werry next day, as I always goes to see about Christmas time, as lives close ag'in Portland Place, tho' not in tho grand 'ouse as she did used to 'ave in Sir Samuel's lifetime.

Ah! that were a 'ouse more like a pallis, with balls and parties as Queen Wictoria might 'ave been proud on, with a perfessed cook, as 'ad two cooks and three kitchen-maids uuder 'im at one time, and never did nothink but the flavourin' and sauces, as would take and throw a saucepan of melted butter slap over 'em if they'd let it bile or the least lumpy, as trembled afore 'im in a rage, with the rollin'-pin at their 'eads, and stewpans a-flyin' about the place like 'ail.

She were a kind soul that Lady Wittles, as ever I knowed, and glad to see me, a-shakin' 'ands that afferble like old friends, and makin' me 'ave cake and wine the werry instaut as I got in, and always calls me Martha still as tho' I were a gal, a-askin' arter Browu as if he'd been 'er own brother, with the names of all the children quite pat, as the sayin' is, and a-askin' arter 'em all.

She give me the five pouuds as she'd doue for ever so many years, as she did used to 'elp me with when we was in low-water, me and Brown, and would keep it up when we didn't want no 'elp, for me to give away.

I 'ad my dinner with 'er lunch, thro' bein' all alone, 'cos iu a gen'ral way I always 'ad diuncr in the 'ousekeeper's room, leastways in Mrs. Johnson's lifetime, as lived with 'er thirty year, but thro' 'er bein' dead I didn't care about strangers.

I was a-tellin' Lady Wittles all about that Wait as couldn't keep from larfin' at me about the flower-pot, but says, "Poor feller, he must be 'elped," and sent 'im a sov'rin ag'in the rent, and says to me at partin', "Let me know what more he wants, and I'll 'elp 'im if a worthy case."

So I thinks to myself, that's the best night's work as ever he did with a flower-pot, and took the omblebus from close by Lady Wittles', as put me down at the end of the street as led to where that Wait was a-lodgin'.

I never see people more grateful than they was for the 'elp as I'd brought 'em, as seemed to cheer 'im up, tho' 'is cough were a-tearin' 'im to pieces; and when I said as I'd come to 'ave a cup of tea with them, as 'ad brought 'arf a pound with me, they was pleased, with a fancy loaf, and some fresh butter with 'arf a pound of cooked 'am, and some eggs, as I got the boy to bring where I bought 'em in Walworth, I thought as she'd 'ave 'ugged me.

He was a-settin' up tho' werry weak, but scemed to relish 'is tea, and were a-showiu' me certifycits as he'd got for good behaviour and that like, and said as 'is friends was respectable in the country, and 'is father well to do as 'ad retired from the 'orn business, but as he didn't like to ask 'im for nothink, thro' 'avin' parted in hanger all thro' 'is brother's wife.

"Well," I says, "never you mind your brother's wife nor nobody's else's but your own, as is your duty, and make it up with your father," I says.

His wife 'ad stepped out for some milk and sugar, and I will say was as neat as print, and the room that fresh tho' a bed in it; so when she come in we talked it over, and afore I left 'em with enough to buy their Christmas dinner, he'd wrote the letter, and a beautiful letter too, as show'd the scolared all over.

Two weeks arter Christmas they both come over to see me dressed that respectable as nobody wouldn't 'ave know'd 'em, and the little boy too in black.

I was glad to see 'em, as told me as 'is father 'ad sent 'im a kind fatherly letter, thro' 'is sister-in-law bein' dead, as they'd put on black for, as 'ad softened 'er 'usban', as sent a post-office order for five pound, as were untold gold to them, and 'ad made 'em all on the square ag'in, and they was a-goin' down to the old man that werry next day.

So I says, "I think as I shall shove a flower-pot into all the Waits' eyes as comes along, for," I says, "it brings good luck," and so it did, for he wrote me a beautiful letter from 'is father's, as were livin' with 'is brother, as were a malster, a-thankin' me.

That man as were 'is mate come on Boxin'-day the wuss for liquor, as said I'd promised 'im a Christmas-box, and when I refused went on that abusive, a-sayin' as I'd pretty nigh murdered 'em both with flower-pots, but the perlicemen he come by jest then, so my gentleman 'ooked it, as the sayin' is, and I never 'eard no more on 'im, tho' I could swear as it were 'im as were a-playin' along with a 'arp outside a public-'ouse door one Saturday night, as is their 'abits.

I 'eard of them Fletchers that werry next summer, as come to see me a passin' thro' London a goin' out to Australier, as 'ad berried 'is father, and was a-goin' for to hemigrate along with 'is brother, as were a-goin' to marry ag'in.

"Well," I says, "I'm glad to 'ear it, for I think as the sea woyage will set you up; cos I could 'ear as he 'adn't shook off 'is cough.

"Yes," says 'is wife, "that's what the doctor says, and so we're a-goin'"

They wanted to pay me back the money as I'd give 'em, as in course I wouldn't take, thro' bein' mostly Lady Wittles, but," I says, "keep it for them as you may meet in distress over there, and give it 'em at Christmas time as will make you remember the old place when you're far away, for," I says, "Christmas is Christmas all the world over, and did ought to be kep' accordin'"

3

"Oh," says Fletcher, "we shan't 'ave frost and snow there, but brilin' 'ot weather at Christmas, thro' bein' the other side of the world."

"Well then," I says, "they did ought to turn it round, as don't seem nat'ral to keep Christmas in summer, as you might as well 'ave snow in 'arvest," as the sayin' is.

I 'eard of them twice over there as Fletcher quite lost 'is cough at sea, and 'er a-gettin' quite stout, and a-doin' well, as I only 'ope may last.

But when you comes to think them poor Waits must 'ave a 'ard time of it, as parties pre'aps might think was as gay as larks, as the sayin' is, a-playin' them merry tunes all night, and all the while 'as 'eavy 'arts and empty stomichs to play on, as can't make no one gay, let alone sickness and sorrers at 'ome, like them poor Fletchers, as 'ad suffered a deal afore I give 'im that shove in the eye with that flower-pot.

So that's why I always gives a trifle to them Waits, and when awake of a night at Christmas time, and 'ears 'em a-playin' I thinks of them Fletchers as might 'ave starved and died but for wakin' me up like that, tho' it's been a lesson to me never to 'ave no loose flower-pots outside the winder no more, as is 'ighly dangerous, as a thoro' draft might carry away, with my bed-room door jest oppersite the winder, as is a reg'lar

current, tho' cool in summer, with a chair ag'in the
door, and me a-settin' out of it for to get cool, as
do not believe in a thoro' draft, not even in the dog
days; and in course at Christmas time would be
certain death, as I'm sure I wonder I didn't catch
a-goin' that night to the winder to them Waits, as I
do believe the fright saved me from, for if ever I
did think as I'd killed any one, it was that Wait with
the flower-pot on 'is 'ead.

II

MRS. BROWN SPENDS CHRISTMAS-EVE.

I MUST say as I likes Christmas time, and always 'as the place cleaned up and the sweeps a good week afore, thro' not a-likin' things drove off to the last, especially my mincemeat, as did ought to be left for to mellow with a good drop of brandy to it, and some do begin their mince-pies Adwent Sunday, as is gone werry much out, tho' I'm sure I couldn't never forget it, not that year for that gal Ann Faulkner, as I'd took out of the parish school for to 'elp, she would go about the 'ouse a-singin', " Clouds Descendin'," till she pretty nigh drove me crazy.

So I says to her, "Ann," I says, " 'ims is werry proper and right in their way, but," I says, "please to remember as you ain't up in the gallery aside of the big orgin now, with your mob-cap and apron afore your face ; but," I says, " now as you're come to service, when you goes to church now you must sing

quiet like a Christian, and not like a charity gal
'owlin' your 'ims all about the 'ouse, as sounds bad
and no religion in it."

Well, I'd got pretty nigh everythink ready
down to my best cheyney out, as we was a-goin' to
'ave friends Christmas-day, and 'ere we was on the
werry eve of it, as the sayin' is, when who should
come in but Miss Masklin, as is more like a 'orse-
marine than a lady, and talks that loud as you may
'ear 'er over the way.

So she says, "I'm sorry as you're engaged,
for," she says, "I came to say as our little charge
ain't so well."

I says, "I'm sorry for it, as I 'oped he might
'ave been 'ere to keep 'is Christmas thro' the family
bein' gone."

"Oh," she says, "I'm sure he won't keep no
Christmas if it ain't put in 'is 'ead."

I says, "Not keep Christmas. Why," I says,
"'ave you been and turned Turk, Miss Masklin,'
for I says, "I've knowed Jews as respected it, and
would eat roast-beef and plum-puddin' jest like
Christians, and as free as if it were the Passover,
as is their Christmas."

"That's what I says," observed Mrs. Padwick,
as were come to stop over Christmas-day, and were
a-'avin' a cup of tea along with me and Miss Matterson, as 'ave knowed better days, and keeps strict

to 'er ehureh, thro' 'er father 'avin' been a westry
elerk, and shook 'ands with bishops scores of times,
as was eonfirmed 'erself in a elear musling froek, a
wail down to 'er 'eels, but always faneied as she
got the rheumatics thro' 'avin' the bishop's left
'and, as they do say is unlucky.

So neither on 'em didn't 'old with that 'ere
Miss Masklin a-runnin' down Christmas, as is a
reg'lar free thinker, as, like drinkin', eomes bad in
a man, but is wuss than disgraeeful in a woman.

For my part I likes Christmas kep' up in good
style, in families partikler, with even the infant
brought dowu to dessert, and the nuss 'er glass of
wiue, as I've see with them as 'ad pleuty for to keep
it with, and so Brown and me 'ave always done in
our little way, tho' 'umble, and would bring me
'ome a bit of 'olly to dress up the place with, tho'
not overmueh in 'is poeket to buy it with.

But as year after year 'ave rolled by things
'ave got easier with us, and as Christmas 'ave eome
round I've 'ad eause to be thankful, as I 'opes I am,
tho' I eould 'ave wished as my boy 'ad settled near
me, aud certingly do not eare about Jane's 'usban',
tho' I ain't got a word to say ag'in 'im as a 'usban'
or a father neither, as to Liza she's that delicate as ean't travel, but well to do, tho' he's too
fond of eatin' and driukin' to be long-lived, in my
opinion, tho' in course that goes for nothink.

I'm sure Christmas is a blessin', for it wasn't nothink but Christmas as ever made old Mr. Mushit forgive 'is daughter as 'ad married ag'in 'is consent, and left a widder with five, and the eldest a cripple, and 'ave brought many a family to it's bearin's, as can't have no 'arts in the right place to bear malice at Christmas time.

So, Miss Masklin she give a toss with 'er 'ead and says, "She didn't see as Christmas had got anythink to do with it, as people didn't ought to bear malice at no time."

I says, "In course not, but," I says, "who on us is perfect I should like to know, and if we've got our little tiffs and tempers, why it's a blessin' as there's a time of year as comes round for to remind us of our duties."

I'm sure I never shall forget that Christmas-eve as froze like mad; with the water-pipes all done up in straw, and plugs in the street for them as were froze out; and I'm sure what with frozen-out gardiners and Christmas pieces, I was a-runnin' to the door perpetual, as is werry aggrawatin' to the temper when busy.

As I was a-sayin', I'd made my mincemeat weeks afore, and was a-bilin' my puddin', as I considers sixteen 'ours ain't too much for, thro' bein' a receipt as I 'ad in the Lord Mare's kitchen, so must be somethink like.

Mrs. Padwick, she'd been busy afore tea, a-
trimmin' up 'er cap, and was a-sayin' what 'undreds there was as didn't know where to get a
Christmas dinner.

"Yes," and I says, "think of the thousands as
will over-eat theirselves, and waste what would feed
them as wants."

Well, jest as we was a-talkin', the gal come
in and said as the copper were a-gallopin' like
mad.

I says, "Let it gallop, as can't 'urt a puddin',
but," I says, "mind as you keeps fillin' it up constant."

She says, "Oh, yes, I've done that," as I
thought I could trust 'er, but says to Mrs. Padwick
as I'd go and see 'ow things was a-goin' on, and
jest as well as I did, for if that dratted gal 'adn't been
and let that copper get red 'ot, and I jest went in to
the back kitchen in time for to see 'er souse in a
pail of water into it, as sent the puddin' sky 'igh,
knocked 'er back'ards with the copper-lid slap ag'in
me, and a mercy we wasn't both scalded to death
with the steam.

I could 'ave cried with wexation, for in course
the puddin's, all but one, was burnt as black as
your 'at, as the sayin' is, and I were that upset as I
felt downright ill, and was glad for to see Miss
Matterson come in, as always talks proper, thro' a

well-regulated mind, as was only to be expected
thro' being that well brought up with 'er grandfather bein' a clock-maker near Clerkenwell Green,
and churchwarden for years, with 'is name in gold
letters in front of the gallery when the church were
repaired and beautified, and was only a-gettin' quiet
in my feelin's when that Miss Masklin come a-
bouncin' in, as ain't a party as is any comfort to
you in troubles, and couldn't make a puddin' nor
'old a needle to save 'er life.

Miss Masklin, she's one of them as is full of 'er
woman's rights, and 'ad come into me about a
month afore, all of a bustle one mornin', to tell me
about that ere little boy a-sayin' as she'd been and
'it the right nail on the 'ead at last.

I says, "Why, what's your meanin'?"

"Oh," she says, "the 'Merrykin women, as
is a mask of genius, 'ave done it, and I'll foller
'em."

I says, "If you follers all as 'Merrykin women
'ave done, or will dare to do, you'll get yourself
nicely talked about, I can tell you. But," I says,
"'ow do you mean to foller 'em?"

She says, "In a-studyin' of medsin."

"What," I says, "walk the 'ospitals like a
medical student, the same as young Smallsted did,
and lodged somewhere near the New Road, and
never come in till daylight, a-'owlin' down the street

with low-lived companions, and pawned all 'is things
for to waste the money at Cremorne, and pulled all
the tickets out with 'is pocket-'ankercher on the
'arth-rug while a-takin' tea with 'is aunt, as is a
partikler Baptist, and told 'er as they was the
numbers of the patients' beds in the 'ospital, and
was sent to New Zealand arter all, and some
thinks eat by them natives, as I pities their
taste."

"Oh," she says, "it ain't necessary as ladies,
tho' students, should let theirselves down to sich
condict."

"No," I says. "I quite agree, with you, and
no decent fieldmale would set among a lot of lark-
in' boys a-'earin' a lecture on sich subjecs, nor
attendin' hoperations, as is only fit for doctors
and nusses."

She says, "Isn't it better as nusses should know
all about it ?"

I says, "No; let 'em foller what the doctor
tells 'em, and not go a-thinkin' they knows more
about it than 'im, and would be sure to kill the
patients off pretty quickly."

She says, "You're werry much prejudiced."

"No," I says, "I ain't. I only says as no
woman, not even at your age, did ought to walk a
'ospital."

She says "One must begin young."

"Then," I says, "you did ought to have begin twenty year ago."

She says, "I didn't come here to discuss my hage with you, but only to ask you to come and see that little boy, as is a patient of mine, thro' 'avin' 'ad esperience."

So I says, "Where do you keep your patients?"

She says, "Oh, I've got 'im a lodgin' close by, and don't think he's so well to-day."

I thinks to myself no wonder, if you've been a-doctorin' on 'im, for she's one of them as fancies she were born to set the world right, and tried to stand me out as there wouldn't be no sickness but for dirt, as we all knows is rubbish.

So I says, "Well, I'm uncommon busy this arternoon, thro' it's bein' jest the time as I begun fires, as in general is Lord Mare's day, or did used to be, as is what I calls a-puttin' it off full late for a bit of fire in the ovenin'," not that Brown and me waited for that afore 'avin' a fire, as we'd 'ad of a evenin' for pretty nigh a month past.

She says, "How you do stick to all them old-fashioned ways, and as to anyone a-keepin' Christmas and sich like, it's downright folly."

I says, "Don't you go to run down Christmas, as 'ave seen you myself take to a mince-pie werry kindly, not despite a bit of my cold plum-puddin',

as I takes a pride in, and 'ave seen 'er take a second
bit when she've dropped in on Boxin'-day, as she've
relished wonderful with a drop of somethink 'ot,
tho' a-pretendin' not to 'old with Christmas, for I
knowed as she were one as boasted iu not a-believin'
in anythink.

Not as she talked that way to me but only once,
and I shet 'er up pretty sharp, for I says, "Miss
Masklin, it seems to me as you believes a deal too
much in yourself to 'ave any room to believe in anybody else."

So as I'd put up my blinds as I were at work at,
and didn't want none of 'er rubbishy talk, I said as
I'd step round in the evenin' when I'd 'ad a cup of
tea, and see that little boy, as she told me 'ad is
knee quite bad.

For she ain't a bad sort, poor old thing! only got
it in 'er 'ead as she's clever, as nobody but 'erself
ever could find out, and like a many of them old
maids as gets soured, liked for to talk more than
she really meant; but, law! what did it matter?

It wasn't much of a lodgin' as she'd took for
that little boy as were a stuffy first-floor back, with
a staircase as were that crooked enough to break
your neck to look up it.

I didn't 'arf fancy the woman as opened the
door as 'ad her front in papers, and a face as were
reg'lar begrimed. She only says, "Fust floor back,"

to me, and walks into 'er parlour a-leavin' me to shet the door, 'as made it total darkness, all but a pane of glass over the door, as adn't never been cleaned in this world.

So I gropes my way up, and stumbles into the room ag'in a tent-bedstead as the little boy were a-layin' in all alone, lookin werry ill.

So I says, "My dear, ain't there no one to look arter you?"

He says, "Yes, mother comes of a night to tidy me up, only she can't stop, 'cos she's got to get 'ome to get father's supper and look arter the rest."

I says, "In course she 'ave, my dear."

"Yes," he says, "she 'as two days a-week washin', as begins at six o'clock, and two miles to walk to it, and baby is only six weeks old."

But I says, "My dear, 'ow come you 'ere away from all the rest?" for I see the poor child were reg'lar down, thro' bein' that lonely.

"Oh," he says, "the kind lady took this lodgin' for me, to be quiet and more hairy."

I thinks to myself she must be a bigger fool than I took 'er for, for it looked into a stable-yard for busses as come in all 'ours of the night, and was reg'lar stifly for drains.

In course I didn't say nothink to the boy, but I begun a-askin' 'im about 'is knee, as he'd put out a-slidin' the winter afore, and 'ad been in the 'ospital with, and come out better, but hád brought it on ag'in three weeks afore thro' a-runnin' with 'is 'oop.

Jest then in come Miss Masklin, a-makin' as much row as a regiment of sojers. "Ah!" she says, "I've told 'im 'ow wrong he was a-wastin' 'is time in idleness with slidin' and 'oops, when he might 'ave been a-improvin' 'is mind, for youth," she says, "is the seasin for improvement, as can't never be recalled."

I says, "If you wouldn't mind a-standin' out of the light, Miss Masklin, I should like to look at 'is knee," for I didn't want none of 'er sermons, as is made to 'ear 'erself talk.

When I come to look at the boy's knee, I see as he were a mask of debility, and wanted feedin' up, and asks 'er what the doctor 'ad ordered for 'im.

She says, "I'm the doctor, as 'ave kep' 'im very low, for fear of fever, with constant poultices."

"Well, then," I says, "the best thing as you can do is to send for a doctor, throw the poultices out of winder, and, if he was a child of mine, he should 'ave a mutton-chop and 'arf a pint of stout afore he were a 'our older."

"Oh dear no," she says, "I've brought him

some semerliner aud a brown bread biscuit, as is fine for the blood."

I says, " I ain't got nothink to say ag'in semerliner, as they do say restored the Pope to 'ealth, so must be wonderful, but," I says, " this child ain't the Pope, as 'ave a fine constitution, no doubt, tho' not a British one; but," I says, " you must have a doctor," and thinks to myself, what's more, you shall, a fanciful old cat, a-tryin' 'er 'speriments on 'uman life like that.

She was werry much wexed with me for a-tellin' 'er it was all rubbish about that knee bein' brought on by 'oops and slidin', for I says, " Do think of the thousands of boys as 'oops and 'ollers too, let alone slidin', and don't get their knees bad." I says, " the boy's a poor constitution, and," I says, "if you don't take care you'll 'ave airysipilis or mortification set in, with your starvin' and your poultices."

" So," sho says, " you'd better mauage the case yourself, as you only finds fault with all I've done, as was for the best," for she was dreadful put out with me for a-tellin' 'er in a whisper that if anythiuk 'appened that boy she'd get 'erself into nice trouble.

She says, " Pre'aps you'ro right, as I should be judged by bigots and fools."

" Woll," I says, " that's as may be, for there's

plenty on 'em about, but," I says, "I shall go to
Mr. Camplin myself, and ask 'im to step in and see
the child at once."

He was at 'ome, as luck would 'ave it, and come
with me, and no sooner see the boy than he said as
he ought to be moved to the infirmary, and said it
were a case of gross mismanagement, as put Miss
Masklin in a nice rage, and if she didn't walk out
of the place in a 'uff.

The doctor agreed with me about givin' that
boy nourishment, and sent 'is own boy back with a
mutton-chop and a pint of stout, as I took and
cooked with my own 'ands, thro' a-borrerin' a grid-
iron of the woman of the 'ouse, as looked like thun-
der and smelt that strong of red 'errin's as I 'ad
to 'old it over the fire ever so long, and took 'arf a
newspaper and a bit of rag to clean it proper, but
the chop were cooked beautiful, tho' a coke fire, as
I can't abear myself, but certingly burns clear.

I never see anythink like the way as that boy
enjoyed that chop, as I cut up for 'im as fine as
blackbirds, and let 'im eat 'is brown bread biscuit,
and drink 'arf the stout, as I give the rest on, with
the top of the chop, to the woman of the 'ouse as
looked starvin' 'erself, and seemed thankful.

That boy fell off arter 'is meal fast as a church,
as the sayin' is, and I set there a-watchin' 'im till
'is mother come in, without wakin' 'im up, a poor,

wore-out lookin' creetur', as told me she 'ad five
on em, and 'er 'usban' often out of work, as she 'ad
often to stand at the wash-tub from mornin' till
night, to get 'em a bit of bread, and was all a-goin'
to hemigrate soon.

So I told 'er what the doctor 'ad said about the
boy a-goin' to the infirmary, as 'ad sent me the
horder.

But she says, "'Ow can I move 'im this
evenin'?"

"Why," I says, "a cab will do it, well
wrapped up, for it's death to 'im, a-sleepin' 'ere all
alone."

"Oh," she says, "I'm come to stop with 'im
all night, and my little gal is a-comin' with the
babby, and as to a cab, the money as I've got won't
run to it."

Jest then the gal came in with the hinfant, and
a remarkable fine child, as that poor little gal
couldn't 'ardly carry.

So, arter a little talk, we agreed as the boy
should go into the infirmary that werry night, if he
woke up in anythink like time, or else fust thing in
the mornin', but as he didn't seem likely to, I went
'ome and left 'em, a-givin' 'er a trifle for the cab and
a bit of coal, for I couldn't have slep' over that coke
myself, not if it 'ad been ever so.

The mother, she come later on that werry

evenin', and told me as 'er troubles was all about that boy, for she says, " We're a-goin' to hemigrate, with our passage paid, and everythink packed, and only the ground to sleep on, with a washin'-tub upside down for a chair, as that ere lady told us she'd get 'im well in a week more than a month ago."

" Well," I says, " get 'im into the infirmary, and we shall see 'ow the cat jumps, as the sayin' is.   But," I says, " any'ow you can't hemigrate 'im with such a leg as that."

" No," she says, " the doctor wouldn't never pass 'im."

" And quite right, too," I says, " as would go and spread them disorders all over the world."

" Law !" she says, " a bad knee ain't ketchin', is it, mum ?"

I says, " Pre'aps not, but rules is rules, and no sickness ain't allowed for to hemigrate."

" But," I says, " you get the cab, and get 'im into the infirmary the fust thing to-morrer, as it's so late now."

She says, " I've been 'ome to see my 'usban', as is a-frettin' 'isself to death about waitin'. "

I says, " That won't do no good; but," I says, " get that boy to the infirmary," as she promises

me faithful should be done as soon as she could
next day.

She called in early the next mornin' arter, to
tell me as he'd been took the infirmary in a cab and
blankets; so I went to see 'im that werry arternoon, and found 'im that clean and comfortable,
with a kind soul for a nuss, as it did my 'art good
to see 'im.

But, certingly, I changed my tune when the
nuss told me on the quiet as the doctor said as 'is
leg must come off.

I says, " Poor little chap; does he know it?"

She says, " No, not yet. Would you mind a-
tellin' 'im ?"

I says, " 'Is mother's the fit person," as I
knowed would be a awful shock to 'er, for they
must leave 'im behind, or forfeit their passage-
money.

While I was a-talkin' to the nuss outside the
ward, in come 'is mother, and as soon as she 'eard
'is leg bein' took faints dead off.

So I says, " Bear up, and think of your hinfant,
for whatever is a leg compared with life ?"

She says, " Yes; but 'ow can I go and leave
'im behind, and whatever is to become on 'im; not
but what," she says, " he might foller with my
sister, as will sail six weeks arter."

" Well, then," I says, " cheer up, no doubt

he'll be all right by that time; and I promises you
when he's out of the 'ospital I'll look arter 'im till
sieh time as your sister sails."

That seemed to cheer 'er up, and she went and
see that boy and broke it to 'im about 'is leg, as
he took quite cheerful and said he should be glad
to get rid on it as 'ad give 'im awful pain.

A day or two arter that he were moved to the
'ospital, and bore the imputation like a reg'lar little
Nero and no cloryform.

He 'ad been a-gettin' on nicely, and took leave
of 'is parents without a tear, as set sail two days
arter the operation.

So I was werry much took aback when Miss
Masklin come in that Christmas-eve a-sayin' as
he weren't so well, for I'd promised 'im he should
come 'ome to me on Christmas-day, with a plum-
puddin' for 'is own self, and a mince-pie for every
one of 'is little cousins as was all ready to sail. I'd
got a bit of beef for 'em, thro' Old Lady Wittles,
as always sent me five pounds at Christmas for to
give away for 'er.

So I was dreadful disapinted to 'ear as he
weren't so well, and as soon as ever tea were over
I set out for to go and see 'im; for I couldn't 'elp
a-fancyin' as that there Miss Masklin wanted to
make out as he were wuss than he really were.

So as I didn't make no company of Mrs. Pad-

wick nor yet Miss Matterson, I left 'em to be
company to theirselves, and tho' piercin' cold I
started; and Miss Masklin, she said as she shouldn'+
go, for she'd wowed never to set 'er foot in that
'ospital ag'in, thro' 'avin' been insulted by both
doctors and nusses, as she were determined to un-
mask the whole lot on afore she'd done with 'em.

As soon as I got in the ward, that little boy was
glad to see me, as said he'd been a-'opin' as I'd
come all day, for he said as Miss Masklin 'ad been
there a-tellin' 'im as they'd been and ruined 'im for
life a-cuttin' off 'is leg, and 'ad made 'im that
miserable, and that he wouldn't be able never to
foller 'is parents nor yet a trade.

"Oh, my dear," I says, "don't you mind what
she says, as means well; but," I says, "she' got a
bean in 'er bonnet, as the Scotch says."

"Yes," says the nuss, "and 'ave been 'ere
a-callin' the place a reg'lar slaughter-'ouse, and the
doctors butchers; and as to me, she says, why,
she said as I were the wust of the lot, and got that
furious that she were told by the 'ouse-surjon never
to come 'ere no more, and went off in a towerin'
rage."

That boy 'ad been about the ward with 'is
crutch over a week, and the doctor said might be
moved easy, not as he would adwise ship-board for
another week.

So I didn't make no more ado, but gets a cab,
and brings 'im away with tears in 'is eyes, a-blessin'
them as 'ad been that kind to 'im in that 'ospital,
as I do believe them doctors 'ave 'arts of gold with
the sick, and I'm sure the nusses there was a good
sort.

I never see a child more grateful than that little
feller, as I'd made 'im a bed in the back parlour,
and didn't he enjoy 'is Christmas-eve, with butter-
toast for 'is tea, and a good bason of arrer-root for
'is supper, an slep' like a top.

He stopped with me till over the New Year,
and then they all sailed for the other world, as
is a long journey, but nothink when you're used
to it.

It was months and months afore I 'eard on 'em,
and then the father wrote, as were a scholard, wrote
and told me as they was a-gettin' on fust-rate, and
as Dick had got quite strong barrin' his leg, as he
'ardly missed, and 'ad been able to climb up the
ropes 'isself a-goin' out, as Dick wrote me with 'is
own 'and as a poscrip'. and said he couldn't believe
as 'is leg were off at times, as I knows is true, for
there were old Cap'n Uxtable, as 'ad 'ad both 'is
legs shot away at Copinagen, he always did used to
complain of cramp in 'is toes; as in course was
gone with 'is leg, as does seem 'ard when you've
lost 'em they should pain you; so in course 'avin'

your leg off wouldn't be no relief for corns, as a times 'ave pretty near crippled me.

In spite of all as Miss Masklin may say ag'in it, if my leg's to come off, give me a fust-rate doctor under cloryform, as you never can tell whether you're alive or dead; tho' I've no notion of 'avin' for a tooth; tho' I can't say as I'm partial to pain; but shall always think of little Dick Abud's leg whenever it's a Christmas-eve.

III.

MRS. BROWN'S CHRISTMAS-DAY.

IT were a bitter cold night as ever I felt that Christmas-eve some seven years ago, and 'ad been cold for days afore—a reg'lar old-fashioned Christmas, folks was a-sayin'; and I thinks to myself as I'd rather 'ave a new-fashioned one, for my part, with all the distress as there was about, and everythink that dear; not but what that's been the same ever since Christmas were inwented, no doubt.

But, law! it seems to strike you more, as the sayin' is, when you sees the shops all set out that gay with all as is good in the grocery line, with prize meat that fat as is downright waste, and werry fine for cooks as sells their own fat, like I've 'card tell of one as lived along with a nobleman as 'ad over one 'undred a-year for 'is grease alone, as was somethink like kitchen-stuff, as many won't allow their cooks to keep, as no doubt often leads to awful waste, with wax-ends and fresh butter throwed in; but ain't nothink to a pig-tub, as will swaller up many a silver spoon, and didn't ought to be allowed not in a airey in London, as brings all the blue-bottles for miles round, and is enough to breed a plague three doors from where Mrs. Padwick did used to live.

I'd been out that 'ere Christmas-eve a-buyin' a few things, not but what I was a-feelin' a little down and discontented, for me and Brown was a-goin' to be all alone Christmas-day, for we wasn't 'ardly friends with Jane and 'er 'usban', tho' Brown 'ad shook 'ands with 'im; and they was the only ones we 'ad near us, thro' Joe bein' in Canada, and Liza too delicate for to come up, and go down there Brown wouldn't, so in course I stopped with 'im; not but what I'd asked Jane and 'er 'usban', as preferred a-goin' to 'is own family.

I'd made my mincemeat, and my puddin's were biled, bein' three, and 'angin' on a 'ook iu the wash'us, as would only take an 'our or so to warm thro'; and I was a-settin' soliugtary thro' Brown bein' at 'is club, when a knock como at the door, and in who should como all of a 'urry but Mrs. Arber, as lives oppersite, and says, "Mrs. Brown, mum, old Mr. Mushit's 'ad a fit, as I found 'im myself with 'is 'ead in the fender not three miuits ago."

I says, "Whatever 'avo you deno to 'im?"

She says, " Nothink but run over for you."

So I calls to the girl to give me my bonnet and cloak, and drawed a old worsted stockin' over my shoes, thro' it bein' that slippery in our street thro' the plug 'avin' busted and overflowed, and froze that werry arternoon all over the place.

I wasn't werry long afore I was in Mrs. Arber's front parlour, as that old Mushit lodged in, thro' bein' as reg'lar a old curmudgeon as ever drawed breath.

The moment I see 'im, as was a-layin' on a old black 'orse-'air sofy, as was that bristly and jest like settin' down on a 'edge-'og, I see as he were in queer street, as the sayin' is, thro' bein' insensible and snorin' like, with Mrs. Arber's little gal a-rubbin' 'is temples with winegar.

So I says, " Give me some brandy."

She says, " There ain't such a thing in the 'ouse, as he'd go mad if I was to buy for 'im."

I says, " He'd better go mad than go dead, as he will do, and ain't made 'is will nor nothink." So I says, " Here's a shillin', fetch some, and go for the doctor."

Well, thro' the Bunch of Grapes bein' next door, the brandy were soon got, and I got a good drop down the old feller's throat, tho' I 'ad to open 'is mouth with the 'andle of a tea-spoon, and see the colour a-comin' back in 'is face ; and by the time the doctor come he was a-gettin' his senses more about 'im.

The doctor said as it were rather a sharp attack, and there wasn't much to be done, but to get 'im to bed, and he'd send in some med'sin, as he were to take at once, and he'd see 'im in the mornin'; but says he to me, "He didn't ought to be left."

I says, "I'll see to that, and you'll look in the fust thing in the mornin', like a good soul," as he promised faithful as he would.

I 'elped Mrs. Arber to put the old feller to bed, as was a-gettin' 'is senses rapid, and by the time as the med'sin come, knowed us all.

He looked werry uncomfortable at seein' me, as 'ad 'ad words with 'im over buildin' a wash'us at the back of our 'ouse, when he did used to live next door to us once, along with 'is little daughter, as I'm sure he always must 'ave cared for, thro' 'er bein' the only one as he'd got alive, as put 'im out fearful thro' 'avin' gone and married ag'in 'is will, and 'is wife died when that child were born, as wasn't under 'is roof, but in a lodgin', as I got that poor woman; thro' 'is temper.

He said as he'd 'ave let that poor hinfant go to the work'us, and only took 'er in to spite 'is wife's father, as wanted to keep the child; but he was always a 'asty temper, and drove 'is eldest son by 'is fust wife to sea, as were drownded in 'is woyage to Cheyney, thro' bein' swep' away by a gale into the Yaller Sea.

I well remembers that child of the Mushits bein' brought 'ome from Margate, where he'd 'ad 'er at nuss till nearly seven; and the way as 'is old drunken 'ussey of a servant, as called 'erself 'is 'ousekeeper, ill-treated that gal were shameful, and did used to set 'er own father ag'in 'er, as were many years older than that poor child's mother, as 'ad always 'oped to berry the old brute as she called 'im often to my face, as is a wrong feelin' in a wife.

If I'd 'ave knowed as much as I did arterwards I shouldn't 'ave took 'er part, and got my lessou then not to interfere 'twixt man and wife, not as ever I persuaded 'er to leave 'is 'ouse.

So when out that Christmas-eve, Mrs. Laurin, at the chandlery shop, was a-tellin' me about 'er, and while we was a-talkin' in she come, lookin' that pale as give me quite a turn, and 'ardly enough clothes on to cover 'er.

Poor thing! she began to cry when she see me, and told me all 'er sorrers, as was 'eavy thro' bein' poverty and sickness, as is 'eavy to bear together.

But I cheered 'er up a bit, and made 'er walk as far as my place, and give 'er a drop of 'ot elder wine, and some in a bottle to take 'ome with 'er, jest a somethink for to 'elp 'em over Christmas,

a-promisin' a puddin' the next day, as I made for
Jane's children; but that father of their'n 'ad told
'is wife as he didn't want wittles for 'is children,
so the puddin' was a-goin' a-beggin', as the
sayin' is.

I was downright glad as that poor Charlotte
should 'ave it, as 'adn't no idea where she were,
'avin' never set eyes on 'er since she married, tho'
it seems but yesterday like as she come from Margate, as I can see 'er now, a poor pale-faced meek-
lookin' child she were, as I did used always to say a
kind word to, with a bit of puddin' now aud then,
thro' 'avin' knowed 'er mother, wheu that old
Witch of Endor of a 'ousekeeper, a wile old 'ussey
as I did used to call 'er, weren't a-lookin'

Well, as I were a-sayin', old Mushit and us 'ad
a row over our wash'us, as he tried to stop our
buildin' it, and come into my place one mornin'
with 'is stick and umbreller, a 'obblin' thro' a
clump foot, and says, "I'll have every bit on it
down."

I says, "Will you? I should like to see you
touch it."

"Oh," he says, "I'll have the distric' surveyor
to you, as will pison me with smoke."

I says, "Will you," I says, "then you'll 'ave
your trouble for your pains, for we'vo squared it
with 'im."

He says, "I won't 'ave none of your washin' and steamin' into my place."

I says, "Who's a-goin' to steam into your place," and I says, "you looks as if a little washin' would do you good."

He takes up 'is stick, and shakes at me, a-sayin' for 'arf a word more he'd lay it over my back and take the consequences.

" I should like to see you dare to, you old dot-and-go-one objec'," I says.   " You walk out of my place," I says, "and if you wasn't a cripple I'd lend you a leg to 'elp you out."

He'd opened the door, and turns round and says, " Ah ! you're drunk as usual."

Well, I couldn't stand that, as was only eleven o'clock in the mornin', and I was a-sweepin' the passage when he come in.

So I says, " I'll sweep you out with the rest of the rubbish, if you don't go."

He turns round, and haims a blow at me with 'is stick, as made me give a drive at 'im with my broom behind, never a-meanin' to touch the old cripple, but he thought as I did, and give a spring like, and pitched all-fours down our steps, jest as Mr. Firkins, the Wesleyan minister, as is a fine full figger, were a-comin' up for to see 'is own sister, as were a-lodgin' along with me, and if old Mushit didn't reg'lar pitch into the pit of 'is stomich, and there they both was a-rollin' into the road.

I never was so frightened in all my life, for I thought as Mr. Firkins were dead, for old Mushit kep' a-kickin' at 'im with his clump foot like a sledge-'ammer on 'is face, as I 'ad to run and ketch 'old on, not afore he'd Mr. Firkins's two front teeth out, as was luckily false, but stopped Mr. Firkins's preachin' that next Sunday, as couldn't say nothink plain without 'em.

What made it wuss was as them two was deadly henemies thro' old Mushit 'avin' been one of the deekins at the chapel as Mr. Firkins preached at and 'ad left thro' not a-'oldin' with Mr. Firkins's doctrines, as he said wasn't free grace. So Mr. Firkins 'ad 'im up for the assault, as got fined thro' the magistrate a-dismissin' the summons ag'in me, as old Mushit 'adn't no right in my place when told to go out, thro' every Englishman's 'ouse bein' 'is castle, as the sayin' is.

From that day me and Mr. Mushit never spoke for years, till 'is old 'ousekeeper, as he called 'er, were burnt to death, thro' liquor, as she were give to, and me a-smellin' her burnin', and give the alarm, as 'ad fell onto the bars, arter beatin' that poor gal nearly to death with the copper shovel, for tryin' to hide the gin-bottle away from 'er.

Old Mushit, he were out when it 'appened, but as I'd saved the 'ouse from bein' burnt down, thro' givin' the alarm, he come to the door, and said as he should like to shake 'ands, and so we did.

But arter that I know'd as he led that poor daughter of 'is'n a fearful life, as would never let 'er out of the 'ouse, and threatened as he'd beat 'er with 'is crutch till she couldn't stand if she moved, so it's no wonder as she bolted with the young feller as were a plasterer and son to the widder at the coal-shed round the corner afore she was seventeen.

That old feller come in to me when she'd lewanted, to try and find out if I'd 'ad any 'and in it, as said I knowed nothink of 'er, and no more I didn't.

Well, he wowed everlastin' rage ag'in 'er, and took 'isself off, and as he didn't want no more 'ousekeepers burnt to death, give up 'is 'ouse and went to lodge oppersite with Mrs. Arber, as I always did think were a-settin' 'er cap at 'im; but, law bless you! he was a deal too wide-awake for that.

Well, when he was took with that fit, Mrs. Arber she were up to 'er eyes a-gettin' ready for Christmas, a-cleanin' and all manner, as always were a party to put things off to the last. So she says to me, " Wherever can I get a nuss for him, or I can't set up with 'im ?"

"Well," I says, "there's Mrs. Challin, but I know she's engaged, and so is Mrs. McDonnel."

She says, "Whatever shall I do?"

"Well," I says, "he mustn't be left, as might 'ave another fit and die, and shouldn't never forgive myself, as would look like me a-bearin' malice. So I'll stop with 'im to-night, if you'll send over for my nightcap and things as I wants, and a thick shawl, and leave word for Brown not to expect me."

Well, she got me everythink, and we lit a fire in the old feller's room, as were werry 'eavy and drowsy-like, and when I'd made 'im as comfortable as I could, I set there arter a bit of supper with a little drop 'ot, a-watchin' 'im with a Child's night-light in a sarcer and a good book in case as I should feel inclined to it.

He slep' on till 'ard on three, when, jest as I were a-puttin' on a bit of coal with my fingers, thro' not a-wishin' to make no noise, and the night a-turnin' that cold, as it will do afore mornin', I looks round and see old Mushit awake a-starin' at me with all 'is eyes, as the sayin' is.

I says, "Mr. Mushit, sir, 'ow do you feel yourself by this time? Would you like a little drink?"

He says, "What are you a-doin' 'ere, as knows I'm in my own bed?"

"Yes," I says, "and I'm thankful to see a

deal better than you was many 'ours ago, as I can see by your eyes."

He says, "What have I done to be pestered with you?"

"Well," I says, "I don't know about your bein' pestered, but," I says, "you've been ill, and I've undertook to set up with you."

He says, "Go home to your 'usban'."

I says, "I shall when you're better."

He says, "There's nothink the matter with me. I'm quite well." And if he didn't try to get out of bed.

I says, "Lay still, that's a good soul, or you'll be wuss."

He says, "You don't mean to say I've been so ill as to want to be treated like a child?"

"Well," I says, "Mr. Mushit, I will not deceive you, for," I says, "tho' better, you've been a deal nearer death's door than I considers safe for any one to be without kuowin' it."

He says, "Whatever do you mean? I'm not seriously ill, I know. 'Ave I 'ad a doctor to me?"

I says, "In course you 'ave Mr. Champlin, as says you must be kep' quiet, so," I says, "don't talk no more, but go to sleep."

He says "I can't sleep, and I'll speak my mind. Mrs. Brown, you'ro a woman as I never did like, for," he says, "you've caused me many sorrers, but," he says, "I believe as you'll tell the truth. Am I dyin'?"

"Well," I says, "I 'opes not, but," I says, "what do you mean by sayin' I've caused you sorrers. I don't know as I ever did, except unawares."

"Oh," he says, "never mind that. I only wants to know whether I'm dyin', that I may make my will, as is all I've got to do, so as that young 'ussey shan't get a farthin' of my money, cuss 'er."

I says, "Mr. Mushit, I ain't no parson to preach, but," I says, "how dare you 'ave them feelin's towards your own flesh and blood when 'overin' 'twixt life and death."

He says, "I never did anyone any 'arm, and 'ave paid my way, and 'ave met with black ingratitude."

I says, "You may 'ave paid your way, as is all werry right, and," I says, "as to gratitude, no one expects that but fools; but," I says, "do you mean to look me in the face and say you never did anyone any 'arm."

He says, "Yes, I can lay my 'and on my 'art and say so; and defy you to say as I 'ave, and," he says, "if you think so, tell me, as am a man of my word and 'ave always kep' it."

"Well," I says, "that's all werry well in its

way, but ain't everythink, but," I says, "if you
wants to get well, you must lay down and be quiet,
and not talk no more."

He says, "What's the use of talkin' like that.
I tell you I can't be quiet. I want to know what
you've got to say ag'in me."

Well, I see as he were a-gettin' escited, and
as contradictin' 'im ouly made 'im wuss, so I says,
"Mr .Mushit, I ain't got nothink to say ag'in you,
leastways, escept as you wasn't neighbourly over our
wash'us, as is all forgot now, but," I says, "what I
wants is for you to be at peace with all the world,
as is all our duties, and 'ere is Christmas time for to
remind us on it."

He says, "I never made no fuss over Christmas, as I considers rubbish."

I says, "You'd 'ave been none the wuss if you
'ad, and might 'ave 'ad a 'appy 'ome now, with your
children round you, and smilin' 'appy 'arts." I says,
"Don't give way to them 'ard thoughts, but try to
spend this Christmas as may be your last, as you
did ought to."

He says, "I ain't nothink for to reproach myself with; others 'as treated me bad. I know
that."

I says, "And 'ow 'ave you treated them?"

He says, "I've done my duty; tell me if I
ain't. Don't think as I am tryin' to deceive my-

self, speak out, I'm not afraid to 'ear the truth, nor yet to die neither."

Well, I didn't want to escite the old man, but felt as he were a 'ardened old wretch, and that I should be as bad as 'im if I let 'im die like that.

So I says, " Mr. Mushit, do you really mean to say as you thinks you've done nobody no 'arm." I says, " Try and think."

He says, " You tell me, and I'll thank you if anyone can say a word ag'in me."

" Well," I says, " the world do say as you wasn't overkind to your fust wife."

He says, " She was thoughtless and extravagant."

" Well," I says, " 'avin' never knowed 'er I cannot say ; but," I says, " 'ow about your second ?"

He says, " She disobeyed, and defied me, and I shet my door in 'er face."

" Yes," I says, " and would 'ave let 'er dio in distress, and never said as you forgave 'er tho' she sent for you to come, and then," I says, " 'ow did you treat 'er child?"

He says, " Took 'er from the work'us."

" Yes," I says, " 'cos the law compelled you ; leastways 'er grandfather would, and you only took 'er to spite 'im."

He was a-goin' to speak, but I stops him,

sayin', " Mr. Mushit, you've treated that gal awful
bad, and let that wicked old woman set you ag'in
'er."

He says, " She was always a-deceivin' me, like
'er mother, as you 'elped in 'er artful ways."

I says, " Mr. Mushit, never. I am sorry as I
didn't persuade 'er to stop in your 'ouse that time
as Charlotte were born, but," I says, " I 'ad no
'and in deceivin'."

He says, " Mrs. Gronin said you did."

I says, " That woman was a mask of deceit, as
come to 'er end thro' gin, and told you lies about
every one, as can be proved, and set you ag'in your
wife and child too, for tho' a bad temper, I don't
think as you would 'ave been 'arf so bad if it 'adn't
been for that old wixen, as wasn't nothink better
than a wicked old faggit, as is gone to 'er account,
and did used to beat 'er like stock-fish, poor gal."

He says, " She's been and disgraced me by a-goin'
off with a low waggerbone, and I won't forgive 'er."

I says, " That was better than bein' on the
streets, as that woman would 'ave drove 'er to.
Now," I says, " you listen to me. You're most
likely on your death-bed, and 'ave 'ad time give
you to repent, and don't you lose it."

He says, " I've always been reg'lar to my
chapel till that Firkin's were elected ag'in my
will."

I says, "I ain't got nothink to do with your chapel, all as I've got to say is, as you used your wife and your child werry unkind to my certing knowledge, as I'm sure you never learnt at chapel to do wrong, and it's your own fault and wicked temper."

Now I says, "Don't deceive yourself, for you knows as well as I do as church nor chapel neither won't save any one as neglects their duties," and I says, "that gal's a-starvin', with 'elpless babes and a sick 'usban', as I've 'eard this werry day; now," I says, "save them, or else," I says, "woe betide you."

He looked werry queer at that, so I says, "Now do be quiet for a little." I give 'im a little weak brandy and water, and arter that he dosed off, and seemed to start like now and then.

I set a-watchin' 'im for ever so long, and 'eard the church-clock strike five werry loud, as seemed to disturb 'im, and up he jumps in bed, a-lookin werry wild, and says, "Where is she?"

"Where's who?" says I.

"Why," he says, "my poor Charlotte, as wa 'ere jest now?"

I says, "You've been a-dreamin', she ain' 'ere."

"Oh," he says, "Mrs. Brown, is that you Call Charlotte, I want 'er."

I says, "Lay still, that's a good soul, she shall come in the mornin'."

He says, "I want 'er now. Pray let me see 'er."

I says, "You shall, if you'll be quiet," for I see the tears a-rollin' down 'is cheeks, so I put 'is 'ead more comfortable like on the piller, and off he dropped.

I think he must 'ave slep' over 'arf a 'our, when he woke up ag'in, and says, "What's to-day?"

"Why," I says, "Christmas-day."

He says, "Is it daylight?"

I says, "No, not yet; but," I says, "do try and sleep ag'in, that's a good soul."

He says, "I can't."

"Well, then," I says, "'ave a cup of tea, as I'm a-goin' to make one for myself."

He gives a nod; so I wasn't long a-gettin' 'im a cup of tea, as seemed to warm 'im like; and when he'd took it, he says, a-speakin' werry low, "Mrs. Brown, I wants you to do me a favour. Will you?"

I says, "In course I will. What is it?"

"Why," he says, "I wants you to go and find out that poor gal of mine, and bring 'er to me this werry day."

I says, "That I will, with pleasure, as soon as it's daylight."

He says, "Take my keys, as is in my right-'and trousers pocket, and open that top drawer, and iu the corner you'll find some money; take it to 'er, and tell as I forgive 'er;" and he busts out a-cryin' like a child.

I let him 'ave 'is cry out, as I kuowed would do 'im good, and went to the drawer and found 'is money, as were over seven pounds in gold and silver, in a leather bag.

So I goes up to the bed, and says, "There's seven pound nine 'ere. What shall I take 'er?"

He says, "Take it all, and see as they've got what they wants; but let me see 'er as soon as you can."

"Now," I says, "if you'll go to sleep, you'll be better able to see 'er; so do, that's a good soul."

He took 'old of my 'and, and nodded to me, so I turned 'im round, and he soon fell into a dose, and I set there a-watchin' 'im, a-feelin' thankful as he'd come round like that, for, to give the devil 'is jew, as the sayin' is, he certingly 'ad always been werry straightfor'ard about money, and 'ad got soured in 'is temper thro' bein' jealous of 'is second wife, and no doubt there was faults both sides.

If it hadn't been for that old Gronin' as wanted 'im to marry 'er, he wouldn't never been so 'arsh on that gal, as was one of them as never could

take 'er own part, and was that afraid on 'im as no
doubt she did deceive 'im, as is the reason why
parents didn't ought to be too sewere, as leads to
drivin' children into falsehoods thro' fear, as will
make any one tell a lie to awoid the stick.

Mrs. Arber come in about 'arf-past six, and
took my place, so I went 'ome; and a bitter mornin'
it was, and Brown were a-espectin' me, and 'ad
jest got down; so he made the breakfast while I
was a-dressin' myself, and I must say as I did
relish my meal, as am a good 'and at settin' up,
and was that pleased at that old man a-comin'
round like that.

Brown says, "I shall believe it when I sees 'im
a-doin' what's right by 'is child."

"Well," I says, "seein's believin', and there's
the money as I'm a-goin' to take to 'er almost
directly—not as she's in downright want," for I see
'er only yesterday arternoon, and give 'er a bit of
meat and some tea and sugar, and she's a-goin' to
send 'er eldest boy, as is just past ten, with a
basket for that puddin' as I'd made for Jane's
children.

For I'd agreed with Charlotte as he was to
fetch it 'ot, thro' 'er 'avin' no pot to bile it in, and
only lived in Walker's Buildin's, as ain't ten mintues'
walk.

I started soon arter breakfast to go there, and

called over at Mrs. Arber's on my way, and found as old Mushit 'adn't woke up but jest for a minit, and 'ad took some beef-tea along with 'is medsin, and was off ag'in.

So, as there wasn't no 'urry, I waited a bit so as to give that poor soul a little time to get 'er place a little straight, as with five children and a sick 'usban' 'ad 'er 'ands pretty full of a mornin', and that tidy as she wouldn't like to be caught up to 'er eyes in a mess.

It was werry pleasant, as I were a-walkin' there, for to see such lots of dinners a-goin' to the oven, and parties a-goin' to church as looked well-dressed and 'appy. Some'ow, it didn't seem like Sunday mornin' esactly, but more jolly like.

I can't think, for my part, what parties can be a-thinkin' about as wants bakers not to bake no dinners of a Sunday, as is the only chance many a family 'as of gettin' a 'ot meal once a week; but parties as is well to do in this world don't think much about them as ain't so well off as theirselves; but that's the way of the world, that is.

Walker's Buildin's ain't much of a place for to live in, tho' the rents is tremenjous 'igh, and that poor Mrs. Walford, as were Charlotte's 'usban's name, she paid 'arf-a-crown for a front kitchen, as I will say she kep' like a pallis for cleanness, with a staircase as dark as Newgate.

She was a-washin' the babby when I got in, as were 'er last job, and all the rest was that tidy, with the eldest gal a-readin' to 'er father, tho' I'm sure he couldn't 'ear nothink for that babby's screams, as, like the rest on 'em, couldn't bear 'is clothes on, as in course when you come to think ain't Natur arter all.

Walford was a-settin' there a shadder, for he'd been down with fever and ague for months, as he'd been and caught over a job as he got down in the country at the end of the summer, thro' bein' a plasterer a-workin' at a gentleman's 'ouse over a fortnight, and bad lodgin's in the willage, with ague about as he 'adn't never been able to shake off, thro' wantin' good livin' to get up his strength ag'in.

I'd 'eard of poor Charlotte jest the week afore Christmas, as she were down with fever and werry bad off, but didn't know where she lived till Christmas-eve, as told me she'd got everythink pawned, and only the money from 'is club to live on, and 'ad been obligated to go into the 'ouse when the little boy was born, as were jest two months old.

It's downright wonderful 'ow some poor people do manage for to struggle thro' things, and she'd bore up wonderful, tho' very weak, and quite upset when she sec me come in. So I waited till she'd got the babby off to sleep afore I said a word about 'er father; but tho' I broke it werry gentle to 'er as he'd come round, she werry nigh fainted away when I said as he wanted to see 'er.

But she bore up, and took and throwed 'er arms round 'er 'usban's neck, a-sayin', "Dear Tom, our troubles is over now," as cried like a child, thro' bein' that weak, but was soon better when I give 'er the money to send up to the landlady, as was five weeks she owed, and 'ad threatened to turn 'em out that werry mornin', when she see the dinner, a-sayin', "if they could buy roast beef for Christmas, they could pay 'er."

So, arter a little talk, we agreed as Charlotte should come, and see 'er father at once, and get back to dinner by one o'clock.

I'd got a cab as I kep', and we took the eldest boy with us for to bring back the puddin' from my place, and Charlotte would call at the oven for the beef 'erself, as I know'd was a nice bit, tho' not over fat, with taters and a puddin' under it.

When we got back to Mrs. Arber's, Mr. Camplin 'ad jest been up there to see 'im, and says to me, "He's rallied wonderful, but is werry anxious for to see you ag'in, and says he will get up, as won't do 'im no 'arm."

Mrs. Arber is a clean creetur, and 'ad managed for to send for the barber to shave 'im, as 'ad let 'im wash 'is 'ands and face; so, when I went into the room, he was lookin' more 'isself like.

The fust words he says was, "Is she comin'?"

I says, "She's 'ere."

He says, "Let me see 'er—let me see 'er, this werry hinstant."

I only jest stepped back, and there she were behind me, as fell into 'is 'arms, a-sayin', "Forgive me. I'm a wicked, bad child."

In course I didn't stop to listen, but could 'ear 'em both a-sobbin', as I was in the next room, with only the petition atween us, as ain't no thickness to speak on.

It wasn't werry long afore she come into the room, with 'er eyes werry red, and says, "Father won't rest till he's seen Tom and the children, as he says must come 'ere and 'ave dinner, as Mrs. Arber 'ave told 'im she's got plenty of in the 'ouse for all, thro' 'er own sister a disapintin' 'er, as is only able to come to tea."

"Well," I says, "my dear, let 'im 'ave his way, in course."

Jest then I 'eard 'im callin', and goes in to 'im, and he says, "You and Brown must come and dine too, as I knows you're all alone."

I says, "You must excuse us, Mr. Mushit, sir, as am sure we shall be 'appy to look in arter dinner;" a-knowin' well as Mrs. Arber's table

would be full, and Brown would rather 'ave 'is
dinner at 'ome on the quiet.

So I packs Charlotte off for to fetch 'er
'usban' and children in the cab; and says the
puddin' will keep to eat cold to-morrer, or fried
if you likes it better. And then I went 'ome
at once, but couldn't 'ardly get Brown to believe
as that old man 'ad come round like that, not
as he'd 'ear of goin' to dinner with 'im, as 'ad
got our own dinner at 'ome, and one as likes, as
fine a fowl as ever I see, with a bath chop, as
they calls it, and a nice little puddin' to ourselves;
for the gal 'ad got 'er mother and little brother
a-dinin' with 'er, as 'ad a puddin' to 'erself with a
roast leg of pork, as were a picter, and what they'd
chose for theirselves.

I must say as it were a reg'lar picter, a-goin'
over to Mrs. Arber's to tea that arternoon, as I
would, tho' freezin' sharp, and Brown said as he'd
look in later on, as were as well, pre'aps, for I
don't think as the old man could a-bear the
baccy. No more he couldn't, as it turned out,
but was a-settin' up with a piller at 'is back, all
smiles, with the little gal a-settin' at 'is feet
on a stool, and Charlotte and the babby at the
side on 'im, and 'er boys settin' near 'er with Tom
opposite, with another, and all enjoyin' theirselves
with oringes and nuts. Not but what I could see

as poor Tom Walford were werry weak and trembly,
and couldn't 'ardly keep 'is tears down.

When I got in, Mr. Mushit says, " Here's our
best friend, as 'ave made us all 'appy, thro' tellin'
me the truth."

I says, "Law, Mr. Mushit, sir, I'm sure you
knowed it all well enough yourself, and like a-many
on us, only wanted a-remindin' on it, as is what I
says is the use of Christmas and sich times a-comin'
round."

" Yes," he says, " but many Christmases are
come round to me, but never sich a one as this, as
I might never 'ave noticed but for you."

" Ah," I says, " we've all got our faults and our
failin's ; but," I says, " no doubt we've all got our
chances give us of correctin' on 'em, if we only
takes adwantage of it, as is the werry best thing
as we can do when Christmas comes but once a
year, as I 'opes may be a merry one to you all."

Brown he come in and stopped to supper, not
as we let old Mushit set up, as were werry tired
and ready for bed, and lived over four years arter
that, and left Charlotte a pretty property in 'ouses
out Dalston way, as Tom looks arter, and then
always gives me a look in about Christmas time, thro'
never a-forgettin' the 'and I'd 'ad in bringin' that
old man round, as is the use of afflictions werry
often to bring us to a better mind, as the sayin' is.

IV.

MRS. BROWN AT THE PANTOMIME.

I SHOULDN'T never 'ave gone to that pantermine but for that Sammy as is Mrs. Pilkinton's youngest, with blue eyes and flaxen 'air, as reminds me of my Joe when a boy—not but what Joe were a far finer child of the two, and never give way to like that Sammy, tho' I must say a engagin' child and a wonderful listener, as would set a-starin' at me with all 'is eyes, as the sayin' is, and ask questions by the bushel, and would 'ave it as I'd promised for to go to the pautermine with 'em, as I'm sure I never recollected sayin' nothink of the sort; so iu course I couldn't say 'er nay, though it went ag'iu tho grain, as the sayin' is, when Mrs. Pilkinton she come iu all of a 'urry, two days afore Christmas, and says to me, "Do come to the pantermiue, Mrs. Brown."

I says to Mrs. Pilkinton, "Mum, I will go with

pleasure, thro' 'avin promised Sammy, leastways
he says so, if there ain't no rope-dancing nor
tumblin', nor nothink of that sort, as I always
considers is dangerous to 'uman life, let alone the
limbs, and 'as proved the end of many, the same
as I've 'eard my dear mother speak of a Italian
lady as did used to balance a scaffold-pole on the
bridge of 'er nose, and 'ad it crushed at last thro'
'er 'usban' a-lettin' it down too sudden with a
crash afore she were ready for it.

That's why I can't abear the sight of them
things, as always gives me a turn, partikler since
that time as I know'd that poor gal as fell off the
rope a-dancin' at Stepney fair, as I'm glad they've
put down, as was nearly as bad as Brook Green
when I were quite a little gal, where the London
thieves went down in a gang, and plundered every
one for all the world like the roughs t'other day
with the Militia in the Kingsland Road, and tore
the ear-rings out of Mrs. Pilkinton's aunt's ears, as
was only jest married, and beat 'er black and blue,
and left for dead in a ditch tho' picked out by the
'orse patrol as 'eard 'er groans in the dead of the
night, and was give over by seven doctors round
'er bed, and yet lived to be over eighty-five in
spite of all as they did to kill her.

I never did see a pantermine, tho' I'd 'eard a
deal about 'em, for I did used to 'ear Mrs. Pudsey

talk about 'em a deal thro' 'er 'usban' bein' a stage
carpenter, as never got 'is reg'lar rest for weeks
afore Christmas, thro' a-gettin' that pantermine
ready, as were tremenjous work, with dozens of
children as was paid a shillin' a night for to be tied
up like fairies as 'ad better been in bed, poor things,
as give 'em fearful colds and stiff necks, and I don't
believe as never no fairies could 'ave 'ad sich colds
in their 'eads as Mrs. Gamuck's three gals, as the
eldest weren't nine, or they'd never 'ave gone
a-dancin' about on greens in the moonlight in rings,
as they do say was their 'abits in old times, and
as left their marks on the grass to this werry day,
leastways as I've seed with my own eyes out at
Walthamstow when a gal.

But as I was a-sayin' that eldest gal of Mrs.
Gamuck's never were strong, tho' they do say a
sweet dancer, and looked lovely in pink gauze and
spangles, tho' I never see 'er escept a dirty
sloven.

I don't think as ever I shall get the sight of
that poor gal out of my eyes, as I didn't 'ardly
know nothing about 'er escept a-knowin' as they
must be very poor, thro' only a-lodgin' over Mrs.
Pudsey's, as kep' a general shop, and only one
room, as wasn't no bigger than a band-box, as the
sayin' is.

I'm sure I never should 'ave been in it but for

Mrs. Pudsey a-fetchin' me that night as the poor gal died, as 'ad 'ad a dreadful fall thro' a trap-door, I could see, and couldn't die easy in the 'ospital where they'd took 'er when she fell thro' in the pantermine, thro' bein' a fairy, as were left open thro' carelessness, as might 'ave been the end of all the lot.

I'd often noticed 'er, poor gal, a-goin' out early with 'ardly any clothes to 'er back that bitter weather as we 'ad that Christmas; and as to 'er shoes, they was reg'lar rags. I 'adn't no idea as she were a dancer, tho' at the theayter, as I'd 'eard say was paid thousands and rode in their carriages with lords and dukes a-bowin' down afore 'em, as the sayin' is.

Well, when Mrs. Pudsey fetched me, she told me all about 'er, and said as she 'adn't the 'art to say nay to 'er bein' brought back 'ome there, tho' she says the 'ospital is the best place for 'er.

"Oh," but I says, "a cold place for to die in."

The moment as I see that poor thing, I see as there wasn't no 'opes for 'er, and Mrs. Pudsey, she says to me, " I can't give no time to 'elp 'er mother with 'er except of a night, so will you watch 'er a bit this arternoon, for that poor woman's wore out ?"

I says, "I will," for as to 'er mother, she worked 'ard at that theayter too at the dresses, and was that poor starved creetur as 'adn't 'ardly no life in 'er.

I says to 'er, "What do the doctor think?"

"Oh," she says, "he said as she'd die iu beiu' moved from the 'ospital, as were wrong, you see."

"Ah!" I says, "they knows a deal, them doctors, but not every think;" but I see as that poor thing were done for, as proved true, tho' she did linger over three weeks, and I never see any-think more kinder than them actors was to 'er as did used to come and see 'er pretty nigh every day, partikler one party with a werry wide moutl and a 'oarse woice, as did used to try and cheel 'er up with a pen'orth of bull's eyes, and said as she'd be a-dancin' ag'in at Easter, but were wrong, for she was berried on a Hash Wednes day, and they all follered 'er, and what's more made up the money among theirselves so as she shouldn't be berried by the parish, tho' I'm sure poor souls, they didn't look as if they'd much to spare theirselves, partikler that one with the wide mouth, as they said were a clown with a sick wife 'isself, as cried like a child over 'er grave as they throwed flowers into, poor dear, as were well out of a 'ard world; as ain't no joke even for them as dances thro' it.

So that's why I've always 'ad a 'orror of them pantermines, and 'ave felt thankful as I weren'

born a dancer myself, to 'ave come to my end
sudden, thro' a trap-door pre'aps, as must be a
awful shock to any one's constitution, tho' they
might live thro' it with care.

I must say as I 'ad a misgivin' a-goin' to that
theayter, tho' a day performances as they calls it,
over ag'in Whitechapel, thro' Pilkinton not allowin'
of the children to be out at night, as was all weak
at the chest and wheezy, as I considers is often
thro' a overloaded stomich, tho' Mrs. Pilkinton
were put out at my sayin' so.

I'm sure as it's werry deceptive a-eatin' up
snacks as Mrs. Pilkinton begged of me to come in
and 'elp do, as 'ad 'ad all the family to dinner the
day before thro' bein' Christmas, as was all in the
pawbrokerin' line and well to do.

They must 'ave 'ad a spread by the leavin's as
there was, and all them children 'ad been in to
dessert, as certingly is dreadful spilte, and to see
'em at Margate you'd think was the royal family at
the werry least, with donkeys every day and 'ot
rolls with srimps for breakfast and cold 'am and
marm'lade for tea, as was bein' crammed from
mornin' till night.

I'm sure if ever children was overloaded they
was that day as we went to the pantermine at early
dinner, and 'ashed goose as is a thing I don't 'old
with, for I don't like to eat no one else's 'ashes,

seein' as my own 'ashes don't always agree with me
as will rise tho' you may take jest a thimble-full or
the top on 'em; but goose is goose all the world
over and is better cold tho' requirin' brandy even then

I'm sure I trimbled for to see them children
dewour mince pies with cold puddin' and almon's
and raisins, after a 'arty dinner and bottled ale
with raw chesnuts and bags of biscuits and oringes
to take to the pantermine, as we went to in a cab
as were werry jerky with me in fear and tremblin'
all the way a-watchin' Teddy narrer as were a-ridin'
with 'is back to the 'orse, as never agreed with 'im
oppersite me with my green silk on as I'd 'ad re-
dipped and looked like new.

Glad I was to get out of that cab as seven on
us in weren't no joke, partikler to the 'orse, and
Mrs. Ounsley, as is Mrs. Pilkinton's sister-in-law,
she's a good 'arf cabful all to 'erself any day, and
them four children to fill up with Sammy on 'is
mother's knee a-suckin' 'ard-bake all the way.

She wanted me to nuss 'im, as I says, "No, my
dear," thro' bein' that fond of me as 'is mother
always will 'ave it brought 'im back from death's
door when give over in the measles, and certingly
did persuade Pilkinton to fetch a fisishun at past
eleven o'clock at night thro' a-feelin' sure as he
didn't ought to be bled as the doctor as were attendin' 'im would 'ave done but for me.

It certingly were a noble theayter when we got in and that crowded as we couldn't 'ardly get to our places as were a box as they calls it near to what they calls the stage, and why ever I can't make out, but law! you mustn't espect no sense. in a theayter, as is all make-believe we all knows.

I never see sich a lot of boys and gals as was' all over the place, and as to the nuts, they was a-crackin' 'em all about by the bushel, and a-kickin' up sich a row up above there as we couldn't 'ear a bit of the music for ever so long, till one tune were played as them boys seemed to take to partikler, and if they didn't all sing it together, as sounded werry merry like.

I never see anythink much more darker and gloomier than that pantermine, with creeturs iu green 'eads and red eyes, as come thro' them trap-doors, an' 'ad torches as they kep' a-flashin' about, as I considers werry dangerous, and a bad esample to set children of playin' with fire, tho' in course we all knows as it don't come 'ome to 'em always the same, as the sayin' is, tho' it's right for to frighten 'em.

I couldn't make out what that pantermine meant, tho' they said it were " Babes in the Wood;" but of all the wonderful things it was them demons and fairies a-goin' on, as danced lovely in werry pink legs, with short things on and spangles.

But of all the foolishness it was them babes, as was as big as growed-up parties, tho' a-wearin' pinnifores, with 'eads that large as I says, "Water on the brains!" the instant as I set eyes on 'em.

No doubt that uncle were a bad lot, and so was them that was with 'im, as 'ad hawful faces and spoke werry 'oller, but them children was a mischievous pair as ever I see, and played their uncle shameful tricks, and so they did their nuss, and no wonder he were glad to get rid on 'em as sent 'em away a-embracin' on 'em, and makin' believe as he were werry fond on 'em, tho' they kep' up their tricks to the werry last and tripped 'im up jest as they was a-comin' away.

It give me a turn when they come to that black wood where the two willins as was sent to murder 'em got a-quarrelin' and fought frightful with swords, tho' parties seemed to think it was fun, partikler them two babes as nothink couldn't keep under, for they was a-playin' monkey-tricks all the time as life and death was a-goin' on with them two ruffuns, and that's why in my opinion the one as killed the other left 'em behind in that wood, thro' bein' sick of their ways, and pretty soon made 'em change their tune and werry soon lay down and die.

When they was dead it were werry affectin' to
see them birds, as was a tremenjous size, with
gummy ancles, a-'oppin' on with leaves in their
beaks to cover 'em over, as they did werry rapid
till there was quite a thick bank of 'em, and oh!
sich a lovely fairy come up behind a-standin' on
somethink as joggled about a good deal, and then it
were all changed into a magic bower of floral
delights as they called it, leastways so Mrs. Pilkinton read it to Sammy, as would set on my
knee, and made me trimble for my green silk.

They might well call it delights, for I never see
sich a lot of gas as were a-burnin' everywhere
about, and young gals as was a-layin' all over the
place, and some on 'em a-comin' up thro' flowers,
with birds a-singin' that beautiful as were called
the grand transportation scene, and must 'ave cost
thousands I should say, for the gold and silver was
downright wonderful, not as I cared about it, for
I was all of a twitter for fear as one of them fairies
should get set fire to or go thro' a trap-door, back-
'ards, the same as that poor gal as lodged with
Mrs. Pudsey.

I never see anythink more wonderful than the
way as that 'ere fairy, as stood in the middle, with
one wave of 'er silver wand, changed them babes
as was come to life ag'in into a party as wore lovely
tights, as glittered all over, with a black cap over

'is 'ead and face, for fear as the wicked uncle should
find 'im out, I suppose; and, as to the little gal
as were changed too, she were downright 'eavenly,
tho' rather a stout figger for dancin'.

I never see any one wriggle about more wonderful than that there party in the glittering tights,
as were called Arlekin, and quite dazzlin' to look
at; they called the gal 'is Columbine, as don't
consider proper myself, not but what it was only
make believe, so didn't signify.

Then that fairy took and turned that 'ere
wicked uncle, as come a-sneakin' on, a-lookin' as
tho' he was reg'lar ashamed of 'isself, into merry
Clown.

I says, "He's a nice party for to be merry, a
blood-stained willin with them two babes on his
conscience," as in course didn't know as them
fairies 'ad brought 'em to life ag'in; but law! he
must 'ave been a 'ard 'earted wretch, for he come
on dressed up werry ridiculous, with red and white
'nickerbockers on, an' puttin' 'is 'ands in big
pockets, as went all round, and made werry rude
grimaces at every one, as I consider a bad esample
for children, as I never would allow mine for to
put out their tongues derisive at nobody.

Well, then, he took and turned 'ead over 'eels,
and got up in no time, to give a old party as come
'obblin' in with a stick, sich a back-'ander as seut

'im a-flyin', and then, for to add insults to injuries,
as the sayin' is, if he didn't pick 'im up by the
seat of his pantaloons and knock 'im down ag'in,
tho' I'm glad for to say as he knocked 'isself down,
too in doin' of it. Not as he minded, for he was
up in a instant, and joined 'ands with the old man,
and then Arlekin and Columbine, and they all four;
went a spinnin' round like mad, till it made me
giddy to look at 'em; and then Arlekin and Columbine jumped up ou that merry Clown's back, and
the old feller stood in front, and all them fairies at
the back was all red and blue fire, as looked werry
lovely, I must say, tho' it werry nigh choked me
with the smoke.

Arter that come a street with a pickle shop
and a butcher's, and werry neat fust floors, and
doors with knockers all nat'ral; and in come
Arlekin and Columbine a-waltzin' together quite
lovin' like, as was werry beautiful, but singler
goin's on in the streets, tho' it wasn't much of a
thoroughfare, like them places where the acrobats
shows off, and them two preformin' monkeys as
acts like Christians on a round table.

Well, them two was dancin' together when they
'eard that there merry Clown a-'ollerin' and comin'
down the street, as made Arlekin knock at the
pickle shop and ask the party as kep' it for to
take the young lady in, as were agreeable to; not

as they spoke, but only made signs, as meant pay-in' money.

Well, she wasn't 'ardly gone in, when on comes that merry Clown a-makin' 'isself werry riddiculus, as I wonders he didn't 'ave a crowd arter 'im; but there wasn't nobody but Arlekin, as stood at the back, as was inwisible, Mrs. Pilkinton says. So I says, "Oh, indeed!" for I could see 'im plain enough, and so could that Clown if he'd 'ave liked to, but none so blind as them as won't see, as the sayin' is.

Jest then in come that hold hamberseel, as the French calls it, as 'is name were Pantaloons, as sounded like foolishness to me, for I says to Mrs. Pilkinton, "Why ain't there a pair on 'em to be natural?"

She says, "There is at some theayters, and of Clowns too."

"Oh," I says, "one Clown at a time is enough for me, and I should say too many for them as is down there with 'im, for of all the spiteful wretches as ever I did see, he was one of the wust, for just because that Arlekin as were standin' behind 'im tickled 'is calves with a bit of lath, as he 'ad in 'is 'and constant, and as that fairy 'ad give 'im when she changed 'im, if he didn't take and turn on poor old Pantaloons and give 'im a smack on the face as sent 'im flyin', and then when he got up, ho knocked

'im down ag'in, and kicked 'im over and over, a-
rollin' 'im down ag'in them lights as is in front of
that stage, till I called out shame, as made Mrs.
Pilkinton and all the children bust out a-larfin', as
would stand me out as it didn't 'urt 'im.

I says, "Don't tell me; flesh and blood is flesh
and blood all the world over, as must feel the same
as 'is feller creeturs; but," I says, "in course if that
old man don't mind it, it's no one else's business."

If that old man didn't mind it, I'm sure there
was other parties as did, for I never see a old lady
more frightened than one as 'ad come out a-marketin',
and come out of that butcher's shop with a leg of
mutton in 'er basket, as them two fellers was a-
waitin' for a-'idin' round the corner, and not only
stole the leg of mutton out of 'er basket, but pulled
'er bonnet, cap, and shawl off 'er werry back, as
that Clown put 'em all into 'is pocket, and beat the
old lady shameful about with that leg of mutton, as
run off a-screamin' with 'er bald 'ead.

Next come out the butcher, as bowed and scraped
to them two fellers, and if he didn't let 'em take care
of the shop for 'im, and nicely they went on, a-'ittin'
people about with their jintes, and a-pitchin' the
meat all about the place, and went on that out-
rageous as they was obliged for to bring on a watchmaker's shop and a baccy shop to shet 'em out and
put a stop to it.

I was quite glad for to see that Arlekin and Columbine ag'in as come on and danced lovely afore the watchmaker's, and then Arlekin he dressed up like a sailor, and give us the double 'ornpipe ; but, law bless you, that Clown feller he couldn't let nobody 'ave no peace, for he must come a-botherin' 'im, tho' not wanted, and drove Arlekin away, as always seemed 'arf afraid on 'im, and why ever he didn't take and turn 'im into somethink else with that wand of 'is'n I can't think, for he did wonderful things with it, and changed a clock as was up in the front of that watchmaker's shop, from one side to the other wonderful, and then arter all if he didn't take and jump slap thro' it, as must 'ave been bad for the works, I should think.

But, bless you, that Clown couldn't let 'im do that in peace, but takes and jumps arter 'im, but come a-rollin' out under it, jest in time to kick that old Pantaloons, as 'adn't done nothink, right in the stomich, as reg'lar double 'im up. Not as I pitied 'im, for he was every bit as bad as that Clown, always ready for to jine 'im in any robbery as were a-goin' on.

For jest then some railway porters brought in a large case, as was for the watchmaker, no doubt, but, bless you, them two fellers couldn't let it alone, but must go a-pickin' and a-pryin' into it, and was a-grinnin' together, and a-settin' on

it when a boy comes by with a suckin'-pig on a
tray, and if them two thieves didn't prig it quite
cool, and set on that large case a-larfin' fit to kill
theirselves; but that Arlekin, he was a-standin'
behind a-shakin' 'is fist at 'em, and touches that
case with 'is wand, and if it didn't take and turn
into a kitchen fire, as they was both a-settin' on,
as made 'em jump up pretty quick, as must 'ave
struck 'ot, I should say.

They didn't seem to mind it tho', but set to
work for to cook that pig as they'd stole, as they
put in the oven, and the Clown he took and stirred
up the fire with a tremenjous poker, as he was
werry aggrawatin' with, for he kep' on a-burnin'
Pantaloons legs with it; but was nicely caught at
last 'isself, for if he didn't go and put that poker
red 'ot into 'is own pocket, as made 'im caper about
like mad, till old Pantaloons pulled it out for him,
as were kind in 'im, and like a Christian.

Then arter that them two set down quite friendly
together, and no doubt but what both on 'em was
a-thinkin' they was a-goin' to have a treat with
that pig, for Clown, he were that greedy as he'd
been and licked it all over afore it were put in the
oven, a nasty beast, and then amused 'isself while
it was a-cookiu' with a-makin' slides with a lump
of butter as he'd been and stole out of another
man's basket as come by, and made the place

that slippy as throwed nearly every one down sa come along. I do bate such mischievous ways myself.

But that boy as they'd been and robbed of the suckin'-pig weren't a-goin' to put up with it tbat quiet, and come back with a perliceman for to claim 'is pig, and if tbat Clown didn't say as Pantaloons 'ad stole it from bis 'oner; and I do believe as that perliceman were a-goin' to believe 'im, only Arlekin come behind, and cbanged that there fireplace into a pig-stye; and there was the pigs in it all alive, as Clown ketched up one, and tried to put in 'is pocket and run off witb the boy and the perliceman arter 'im.

Then next there came a garding as parties was a-walkin' about in, and didn't seem at all to see as there was any fun in bein' 'it about and knocked down by that Clown as played 'is tricks on every one, for they 'ollered and screamed frightful, partikler one young lady as come on dressed quite genteel a-readin' a book with a babby in a preambilator.

"Ah!" I says, "that's 'igbly dangerous, and is 'ow the nussmaid come to push them two twins into tho Regency Canal, thro' a-readin' like that."

Well, jest as I spoke, and 'adn't 'ardly got tho words out of my mouth, when she runs the preambilator ag'in that Clown's legs, and caught 'im by

7

the arms, and if he didn't take and set down on
that babby with a wiolent squash. Not as it were
'is fault, I must say, thro' not a-seein' 'er a-comin',
as might 'ave 'appened to myself, or any one; and
in course she did ought to 'ave looked where she
were a-goin' to, a-dawdle.

Well, when he set down like that on that child,
if she didn't run off a-screamin' like a fool, instead
of seein' if it was 'urt; and certingly that Clown
and Pantaloons behaved shameful, for they got
a-squabblin' about that hinfant, and a strugglin'
for it, till they pulled it slap in 'arf; and if Clown
didn't take and cram it into 'is pockets, and then
pitched old Pantaloons back'ards into the preambilator, and wheels 'im off in a 'urry, and jest in
time, too, for a perliceman come in as 'ad been
a-watchin' their goin's on, and springs 'is rattle,
and in comes a lot more perlice, as runs across the
place a-stridin' with all their legs and arms a-pur-
suin' arter them two wretches as fast as they
could go.

I couldn't 'elp a-larfin' myself when that Clown
come in the other side a-wheelin' that Pantaloons
in the preambilator and met them perlicemen as
all tumbled into that preambilator together and
made that confusion, with the young lady a-comin'
in screamin' for the babby as they took piece-meal
out of that Clown's pocket as in course were only a

sham one ; not as people thinks much of a babby's life nowadays.

I were surprised to see that 'ere Columbine as seemed a nice young creetur a-standin' up on Arlekin's leg for to get a good sight on them goin's on from behind and that Arlekin a-shakin' of 'is wand about as tho' they enjoyed the fun.

Well, arter that there were a lodgin'-'ouse as a old lady were a-lettin' a bed-room to them two waggerbones, with their larks, as didn't seem likely as she would to parties dressed that ridiculous without no luggage and no reference neither, partikler as she'd refused that Arlekin and Columbine jest afore tho' she did consent for to 'ide that Columbine in another room as begged werry 'ard when they 'eard them other two a-comin' up.

I must say as I do not consider it were proper the way as that Clown went on arter that, for if he didn't take and open the drawers as was there and take out that old lady's night-things as he put on and then begun for to pull the bed to pieces and bolstered that Pantaloons' 'ead well, and then Pantaloons he got a warmin'-pan from somewheres and took and warmed the bed as Clown 'ad got into, as made 'im spring up like the lark, and tho blow as he 'it Pantaloons in the stomich with that warmin'-pan was enough to have felled a hox, as the sayin' is.

Then if he didn't take and try and warm that
warmin'-pan over the candle, as was a werry sing'ler
candle and kep' a-runnin' up ever so 'igh out of
the candlestick, and then a-sinkin' down ever so
low, as puzzled that Clown, tho' I could see as it
were all that Arlekin's doin's, as 'ad 'id' isself in a
cupboard, and kep' a-peepin' out.

But at last them two got to bed, and Clown behaved that shameful, for if he didn't keep a-kickin'
that Pantaloons out of bed, and a-takin' all the bed
clothes to 'issèlf, a-leavin' that Pantaloons quite
bare.   Not as I pitied that old idjot as didn't ought
to 'ave kep' such company.

Well, they went on with their larks, till at last
they set the bed a-fire atween 'em ; and there was a
hubbub, and lots of parties come a-rushin' in in
their night things, a-screamin' like mad, as nearly
frightened me to death.

So I says to Mrs. Pilkinton, " Let's get out with
the children afore it spreads ;" and up I jumps with
a sudden jerk, a-ketchin' Sammy up, as turned that
awful ill all over me as never was.

Mrs. Pilkinton she quite forgot the lady, as says
to me, " What a fool you must be to jump a child
up like that."

" Yes," I says, " I was a fool to come, but not
such a fool as you must be for to cram a child up to
the brim like this," as it's a-mercy as he were ill or

would 'ave brought on a ghastly·fever, as always comes from a over-loaded stomich.

Well, that poor little feller, he were that awful bad, as we was obligated for to take 'im out to the cloak-room; and I quite pitied the child; but 'is mother were that abusive in 'er langwidge to me, a-sayin' she wished I'd been at Jericho afore ever she'd brought me, as must be a fool not to know as it were all sham.

I says, "Sham or no sham, it ain't no sham as my gownd is spilte."

She says, "And a good thing too, a old dyed thing, as would never 'ave bore daylight, I'm sure, and all your own fault."

I says, "Escuse me, mum, it 'ave took a lovely green, and would 'ave lasted me well till summer, but for your nasty little over-eated brat of a boy."

Not as I felt anythink ag'in the poor child, as weren't to blame, and will over-eat theirselves when allowed; but I was aggrawated with 'is mother, and I says, "It is my own fault for a-comin' to low-lived places in low-lived company; and all as I can say, if you brings up your children on pantermines like that, it's a werry bad esample, as will come 'ome to you some day."

So as the young 'ooman at the cloak-room as rubbed my dress well, I put on my bonnct and shawl and off I went 'ome all by myself, and only

got called a old fool by Brown for a-goin' to such
Tomfoolery.

Mrs. Pilkinton she come to see me the next day
for to apolergize to me like a lady, a-sayin' she were
sorry, as I begged she wouldn't mention it, for
Smith's scourin' drops, as I always uses, 'ad set my
gown all right, all but one place, as don't matter, for
I've got enough left to put in a new 'arf breadth, so
there ain't no great 'arm done, escept as Sammy
were poorly for a day or two.

And no doubt them pantermines is all werry
beautiful and fairy-like, but it ain't a good esample
to children, iu my opinion, to see so much ill-usage
a-goin' ou, as I've see a picter myself of a little boy
as 'ad been took to one a-balancin' a babby on the
soles of 'is feet up in the hair, and nearly a-fright-
enin' of 'is ma to death, while 'is little brother was
a-burnin' 'is grandpa's calves with the red-'ot poker,
as were a-standin' with 'is back to the fire unawares,
a-readin' of 'is paper, as shows 'ow quick some
little people is at ketchin'-up anythink as they sees
done wrong.

But Mrs. Pilkinton, she said as it always made
'er larf to see the children enjoyin' of it, as I must
say is werry pleasant, but 'ow about them parties
enjoyin' of it as is knocked about, as wouldn't do
it unless drove to by distress to get a bit of bread,
as is 'ard lines.

But Mrs. Pilkinton says as them falls and cracks as they gets don't urt 'em.

" Well," I says, " I don't know about that, for I'm sure I was 'urt enough that time as them two young Tuckers as lived in our street run at me full but with their 'eads in the stomich, and sent me a-flyin', as was all thro' their bein' took to the pan-termine, as said as they didn't think as it 'urt fat people to be knocked over," but then all little boys ain't so unruly as them young Tuckers, and of course good boys wouldn't foller a bad esample, not even in a pantermine.

V

OLD YEAR OUT AND NEW YEAR IN.

I says to Miss Masklin, "For my part, I likes
Christmas, and you won't set me ag'in it not if
you was to talk till you're black in the face," as the
sayin' is, as it wouldn't take much to make 'er,
for she's a gipsy all over now, and they do say
as 'er grandmother did used to set cuttin' skewers
under a 'edge out Chigwell way, and told fortins
with a babby at 'er back, and then got set up
by 'er brother, as 'ad been a smuggler, in the
travellin' tin line, as 'ave mats and brooms and
all manner, a-'angin' round their wans, and so
got up in the world, as never told 'er own fortin',
tho' she died rich, but was only tramps original,
as left a only daughter as run away from 'er
uncle's with a doctor's boy, as afterwards come
to be a doctor 'isself, and so she needn't 'old 'er
'ead so 'igh, and go on about Christmas
bein' rubbish, and I says, "If you don't like

keepin' on it, don't; but let others as does alone."

For I knowed as it were all 'er nasty mean ways, as were a-ravin' ag'in Christmas-boxes, a-sayin' they was reg'lar black male.

I says, "You may know more about black males than me, Miss Masklin," as I meant at 'er gipsy lot, " but," I says, "I 'olds with Christmas-boxes, male or fieldmale, as only comes to a few shillins', and makes a many 'appy, not but what some may carry it too far, as I've 'eard say they do over in Paris, and 'ave been knowed to ruin theirselves in them bong-bongs, as is nothin' but sugar-plums arter all, and more likely to ruin 'em as eats 'em than 'em as gives 'em."

Besides, as I were a-sayin' to Mrs. Cleasby last Christmas, "You're as broad as you're long," as is the widder of Mr. Cleasby, the butcher, as kep' a shop, father and son, over forty year, close ag'in Aldgate pump, and never a bad bit of meat in it, for, I says, "you're pretty sure to get it back some way, if not money, why service or civility."

"Yes," she says, "Cleasby 'ave been knowed to give away over twenty pound in Christmas-boxes, as he never begrudged, not as ever he were one for to incourage servants in a-winkin' at false weights nor tainted jintes, nor yet to 'inder 'em

from a-seein' the fat cut off proper, tho' a bit of
flap throwed in with mutton chops a course."

"Ah!" says Miss Masklin, a-plungin' in, as is
'er rude ways, "you're neither on you of the progress party."

"Well," says I, "I don't know what you means
by progress, as werry often is the wrong way, like
them 'Merrykins, as is always a-talkin' about pro
gressin', and werry often finds theirselves a-pro-
gressin' back'ards, as the sayin' is. But," I says,
"if you're so ag'in Christmas bein' kep', Miss
Masklin, whatever brings you 'ere?" for we was a-
spendin' the hevenin' along with Mr. Camplin, the
doctor, as were a-'avin' of a Christmas-tree, thro'
'is good lady bein' brought up among them Germans,
as is given to trees.

She says, "Oh, it's a werry pleasant sight, that
tree all lighted up, with lots of presents a-layin'
about, as is somethink for everybody, as all gives
one another somethink in return, so comes to the
same thing in the end, as I was a-sayin'."

Not as I'd give anythink for that tree, and yet
them young Camplin gals 'ad made me a werry
nice netted thing for to wear over my 'ead, tho' I
'ad sent 'em certingly a jar of my mincemeat, as
I knows is quite equal to the Lord Mare any
day.

I'm sure I never did enjoy anythink more than

that party, as Mrs. Camplin is a motherly woman, and no nonsense about 'er, tho' a 'eavy sorrer, poor thing, I didn't want to come to their party, a-feelin' out of my elephant, as the sayin' is; but Mr. Camplin come over and fetched me 'isself, and would not take nay, thro' a-findin' me alone, for Brown 'ad gone off to see 'is oldest livin' sister near Bristol, as 'ad asked me too, but couldn't give me a bed in the 'ouse, so I says, " No, I thank you, no turnin' out for me at night with such weather as it were, thro' a rapid thaw, as were slush over your ancles.

Brown didn't much care about goin', but as he'd 'ad words with 'is sister's 'usban' over the aunt's will, thought it 'is duty, as is a man as will do it thro' frost and snow, and I'm sure would go thro' fire and water, as the sayin' is, to 'ang 'is own mother, if he thought as he did ought to do it, the same as when he were swore in special constable ag'in the Chartists, not as he ever were one to give in to swearin' ag'in any one, but the way as he kep' out in the streets all that day, with nothink but a penny roll and a savelor in 'is pocket, and never went in for a pint of beer, but drank it on the door-step of the " Catherine Wheel," was the Lord Nelson all over, as died a-doin' of 'is duty, as England espected 'im.

Not pre'aps as England ever espected 'im to be

shot like a dog from the mast-'ead, as didn't ought
to 'ave been there with a-puttin' 'is telescope to 'is
blind eye, as in course he couldn't 'elp, thro' 'avin'
only one arm to 'old it with, as were shot off a-takin'
Gibraltar at the Mutiny of the Bounty, when Admiral Byng were 'ung along with Admiral Parker,
as took part in the Mutiny at the Nore, as were all
about the bounty too ; as I've 'eard a old uncle of
my dear mother's talk about scores of times.

Well, when I'd shet Miss Masklin up about
Christmas, thro' a-twittin' 'er about likin' Christmas fare pretty freely, for I never see any one pitch
iuto everythink as were 'anded round like 'er, and
a-findin' the room werry 'ot and dusty, thro' them
children a-dancin', I walks out into the passage
and sets myself down on the bottom stair, a-thinkin' as I'd go 'ome werry soon.

The door of the little back-parlour were open a
little way, but the room were dark, and as I were
quite close to it I 'eard a sob, and thinkin' it were
one of the children in pain, as 'ad been a-makin' too
free with negus and oringes, or pre'aps some one as
wanted the doctors, I taps at the door and says,
" Do you want anythink ?"

I 'eard some one say, " Who's there ?" and in a
minit out come Mrs. Camplin, with her eyes that
red as I could see she'd been a-takin' on dreadful,
and says to me, " Am I wanted ?"

I says, "No, mum, not partikler, but I do 'ope as you're not unwell; 'adn't I better tell Mr. Camplin?"

She says, "Not for the world; he'd be so angry, and I know it's werry wrong in me to give way, but I can't 'elp it," and she dropped into a chair a-weepin' bitter, a-sayin'; "My poor dear fellow."

I knowed werry well as she were a-takin' on about 'er eldest boy, as 'ad run away to sea, thro' words with 'is father, as is what I don't 'old with any boy a-doin', as in course ain't the Fifth Commandment as come 'ome to 'im, thro' bein' lost in 'is fust woyage jest a year and a arf afore.

I must say as I always did like that boy, tho' a bit of a pickle, and so 'andsome, not as ever I encouraged 'im to run away, goodness knows, tho' he did come and ask me for a cup of tea the evenin' as he went off, and me no more consumption of 'im a-meanin' mischief than the tea-pot as I made it in.

It was ever so long afore Mr. Camplin would believe as I 'adn't knowed somethink about it, till that boy rote 'isself from over there, and said as I didn't, and certingly the best part of that boy was he never told no lies.

Arter all, 'is great fault were as he couldn't abear 'is books, and 'ated the thought of bein' a doctor, as were 'is pa's intentions, as was 'onerable no doubt, as the sayin' is, but in my opinion parents did ought to study a child's disposition, tho' not give in to fancies.

I shall never forget the night as the news come of 'is bein' drownded somewheres near the Red Sea, as a reg'lar place for swallerin' you up alive, and quite as bad as a place they calls the Gulf of Lions were in course no one ain't safe, as the roars can be 'eard for miles.

That night Mr. Camplin come over to ask me to give a 'elpin' 'and with 'is wife, for he said as he didn't think as she'd ever get over it.

I never see a man look more gashler pale, and says, " Whatever is the matter ?"

He drops into a chair, and busts out a-cryin', and says, " Oh, my poor dear boy."

I couldn't 'elp 'avin' a good cry myself, when I 'eard as he were drownded, but I says to Mr. Camplin, " It won't do to give way like this, think of your poor dear wife," as made 'im pull 'isself together; and over we went, and never did I leave 'er for three days and nights, but come round at last, tho' a fearful invalid for months ; but seemed to 'ave got on wonderful during the last six months, as I think 'er mind were distracted with the infant, as were a fine boy.

So I 'ad 'oped as she'd got over it, as 'ad never 'eard 'er name 'im, and Mr. Camplin were werry partikler as no illusion should be made to 'im.

She says, "If I could only see 'im for a instant, to tell 'im I've forgiven 'im, for he was such a good little boy, and used to say 'is prayers to me of a night, and ask me to forgive 'im if he'd done anythink to offend me."

"Well," I says, "never fear, he's asked to be forgiven, and no doubt so he is; and you'll meet 'im in a better world, if you are not to see 'im any more in this."

She says, "Oh, do you think that he may 'ave been saved?"

I says, "Not in this world."

She gave a cry like anyone in agony.

So I says, "Mrs. Camplin, mum, for mussy sake think of your own 'ealth and your 'usban' and family."

She didn't say nothink, but set a-rockin' 'erself in sorrer; and at last she says, "You remembers 'im well, as saw the last on 'im."

So I says, "Come, come, take comfort as you did ought to, as 'ave nothink to blame yourself for."

"Oh," she says, "we were too severe, and Camplin was so angry, and to think I shall never agaiu see my Fred, Mrs. Brown, it breaks my 'art. Ah, he were a fine fellow, and only fourteen," and then she give way ag'in,

I know'd it wasn't no use a-tryin' to check 'er,

for sorrers, like fomentations, will 'ave their way or bust; so I waits a little while, and then she gets out a little case out of 'er pocket, as 'ad 'is likeness in, with a bit of 'is 'air at the back. Such a nice bright lookin' feller, with quite the hair of a sailor all over, as nothink wouldn't keep 'im from the sea, and 'ad made 'is father werry angry, as wished to bring 'im up in the medicinal line; but she says, a-wipin' 'er eyes, "He'd be more angry with me for givin' way like this, but," she says, "the sight of all the rest so 'appy and 'im gone, is more than I can bear."

"Well," I says, "it must be painful, no doubt," and was a-wonderin' 'ow she come to give a party at all, when she went on to tell me as Camplin would 'ave it, and said as the others wasn't to be sacrificed, and it were over a year since he were lost, thro' the wessel a-goin' down on a Red Sea coral reef, as they calls it, somewheres near the Sandwich 'ighlands, as must be a wild spot, for goodness knows it would be bad enough to be lost in them Scotch 'ighlands, like me as is desolate, but no coral reefs nor Red Seas about them as ever I heard on.

Well, poor lady, she couldn't talk to me no more, for she 'ad to go and look arter the young people's supper, as was early, so I goes into the room ag'in, and there was Mr. Camplin, as 'ad been

out for to see 'is patients, as he said to me, eh
always liked to see ex'austed afore the night were out.

"Well," I says, "pre'aps it's as well as they
should be, as might give 'em a good night's rest, as
is a great thing in sickness, tho' in a general way
they often wants keepin' up when exhausted;" as
only made 'im bust out a-larfin', thro' bein' a cheerful party.

Talk of Christmas comin' once a-year, you'd
think as eatin' and drinkin' only come once in a
lifetime, to see Miss Masklin, as went in 'eavy for
cold roast beef and baked potaters, with salad and
bottled stout, besides cold fowl, with 'am arter it,
till I really couldn't 'elp a-sayin' to 'er as I should
be afraid for to take it myself so late, tho' a 'arty
woman in a general way.

She says, "Ah! you're right to live sparin',
you are, with all your corpilence."

"Well," I says, "you needn't talk, for you're
a-bustin' out now at your waistband thro' fat," with
a back as was jest like dough a-risin' over her tucker
as she wore.

She'd no sooner done with the solids than she
went in for cold puddin', mince-pie, and some
jelly, and was a-takin' 'ot punch a-top of sherry,
as she'd dipped 'er beak into pretty free, when,
all of a sudden, she says, "Oh, I feels so faint, as
is my back to the fire."

8

I says, "No, Miss Masklin, it ain't your back as
is in fault, but," I says, "quite different to that,
so come out of the room, whatever you do," and
'urries 'er into the little back parlour, and lays 'er
down on the 'arthrug flat on 'er back.

Mr. Camplin come in all of a 'urry, and says,
"What shall I give 'er?"

"Well," I says, "the best thing as she can
take is some old cheese, as is a fine thing for auy
one as 'avo over-'eated theirselves, for I've knowed
a doctor give it to a man in a fit, thro' 'avin' eat a
leg of mutton and trimmiu's at one meal, for a
wager, and drunk a gallin of beer to 'is own
cheek, as the sayin' is, and dropped down ten
minits arter, as the doctor said Antinomiau wine
would be certain death on a overloaded stomich."

Miss Masklin, she give a gasp and a kick, and
set up a-sayin', "It's false, I'd only jest begun
my supper."

I says, "All right, but," I says, "the old
cheese won't 'urt you, then, as is a find digester,
and a hinnocent thing, as you might give anyone,"
and certingly did save little 'Melia Rice from eatin'
too much cherry-pie, as 'ad dewoured a 'ole one
thro' 'shettin' 'erself in with a table-spoon into 'er
graudmother's larder, and thro' bein' that greedy,
overshot the lock in 'er 'urry, so they couldn't get
at 'er till the door were bust open, and all the pie

MRS. BROWN'S CHRISTMAS-BOX. 119

gone, as she'd been and swallered every one of the
stones, and were found on the floor without 'er
senses, black in the face and kickin', aud the cheese
poked down 'er throat with the handle of a knife.

So Mr. Campliu, he said as she'd better be kep'
quiet any'ow for a bit; and asked me if I'd set by
'er a little while, for we'd got 'er on to the sofy, and
she'd quite come to; so in course I set there, and
puttin' a smellin'-bottle to 'er nose, aud when she
'erself ag'in said, " How could you think as it were
thro' me a 'eatin' too 'arty, as might 'ave been the
jelly as turned me faint, for," she says, " never
could take weal in no shape, and I'm pretty sure
that jelly were calves foot."

I didn't say nothink, but knowed it were all
made of gelintine, as may answer the purpose; but
in my opinion aiu't the thing, for I do believe myself as 'orses 'oofs biled down makes a deal on it,
not as there's any 'arm in a 'orse's 'oof, when you
come to think on it, as can't be un'olesome; and
some says as it don't much matter what things is
made on, so long as they looks and tastes well, but
I always likes everythink clean and 'olesome, and
open and above board, as the sayin' is.

So seein' as she were 'erself, tho' lookin' deadly
pale, I says, " Shall I see you 'ome ?" as only lodged
four doors off.

She said as she thought it would be as well, and

as I were of the same opiuion, I 'elps 'er on with 'er things, and off we goes.

Mr. Camplin he come out to the door with us, and whispers to me as he wouldn't never forgive me if I didn't come back and see the Old Year out and New Year in, as won't be above a 'our more in this world. So I see Miss Masklin up to 'er room, and told the lady where she lodges, to give a eye to 'er, aud let 'er burn Child's night-light; but jest as I were a-goin' out she 'ollered out, and I goes back, as said she were a-dyin' with hagony at 'er chest.

So I 'ad to stop and put 'er on a mustard plaster and give 'er a good dose of sal wolertile aud ginger, as brought 'er round, not as she were in the least grateful, for she said it were all thro' my fault as she were ill, as 'ad been brought on thro' a-comin' sudden out of a 'ot room into the cold hair.

I quite lost my patieuce with 'er, and says, "Rubbish, you've been and eat too 'arty, and take my word for it you'll do it once too often, as ain't no subjec' for suppers, and did ought to kuow better, a-pretendiu' to be a doctor yourself."

"Oh," she says, "yours is the old hignorant lowerin' school. I goes iu for stimilants."

"Yes," I says, "you do, as I considers werry lowerin' for any one to take too much, even at Christmas time."

She says, "If you've come 'erc to insult me,

a-pretendin' to 'elp me, I must beg as you'll leave my room."

I says, " That I can do easy, and wish you a werry good night, and next time as you makes too free at the table, let it be in your own 'ome."

I told the servant gal not to leave till she was asleep, and then as she'd better lay on the sofy in the settin'-room, as were next 'er bed-room, and off I went.

I was a-steppin' back to Mr. Camplin's, and a-thinkin' of the Old Year as were so soon to be over, and New one as were a-comin' in, when a young lad come up to me jest at the door, and says, " Do you live 'ere ?"

I says, " No, thro' it's bein' Mr. Camplin's, the doctor's."

He says, " Yes, I knows that." I looks at 'im in the gaslight, as you can't tell any one werry clear by, thro' bein' red one side and green the other, as always stands for a doctor's, and a great couwenience of a dark night, with any one a-fetchin' 'im in a 'urry, and gives a scream werry near, for if it wasn't Fred alive and 'ome ag'in.

I says, " My dear boy, don't you know me ?"

He says, " Dear, kind old Mrs. Brown, are they all well," and give me a kiss as I 'ugged 'im to my 'art on the door-step.

But I says, " My dear boy, come over to my

place for a bit, for they're all quite well; but you
mustn't give your ma no sudden shock." So without more ado I took and led 'im across the street,
and made 'im sit down in my parlour and give 'im
a little weak brandy and water, as brought back
the life into 'is face, tho' he looked dreadful pale
and 'aggered.

"Now," I says, "I'll go over and fetch your pa,
as 'ave got a little party."

He jumps up and says, "I must see my mother
fust. Oh, let me go to 'er."

"Why," I says, "my dear, you've showed that
sense in not a-goin' in sudden, as I'm sure
you'll listen to reason, and not kill 'er with joy, as
'ave been a-frettin' about you this werry evenin',
to my certing knowledge."

He says, "Do as you like, but I don't think I
can wait 'ere alone."

So over I goes and knocks at the door, and jest
at that instant the clock struck twelve, and the
church bells broke out a merry peal, and as soon
as the door was opened, I walks into the parlour;
there was Mr. and Mrs. Camplin a-kissin' all the
children, and all the children a-kissin' one another,
and a-wishin' a happy New Year all round.

I stopped a minit at the door afore a-beckenin'
to Mr. Camplin, and was a-lookin' into the room
when Mrs. Camplin gave a shriek as went thro' me,

a-'oldin' out 'er harms, and if that sailor boy of
'ern, as 'ad follered me, didn't rush into 'em.

I've see many death-beds often, and 'art-breakin'
sorrers, but never witnessed such a scene as that
were, for Mrs. Camplin 'ad fell back in a dead faint,
and there was that poor boy a-sayin', " I've killed
my mother."

They was all struck dumb like, but I says, " Joy
don't kill, tho' it may give a shock."

I says to the others, as were all crowdin' round
'er, " Leave 'er alone, she'll be better soon," for I
see she were a-comin' to ; and oh ! it was wonderful
to see 'er face of 'appiness when 'er senses come
back, and she give way to 'er tears, and looked up
and see that boy bein' pressed to 'is father's 'art,
as were a-cryin' like a child, and so were the boy,
as kep' a-sayin', " Forgive me for all the sorrers
I've give you."

In course I wouldn't 'ave stayed in the room,
only I was a-'oldin' poor Mrs. Camplin up; but as
soon as she could set up by 'erself, I left 'em
alone for a little bit, and then all the children
was called in to see 'im, even to the baby, as 'ad
waked up with the noise, and wore brought down.

I've see a good deal, but never see sich a picter
of 'appiness as that family, when they all set round,
with the father and mother on the sofy, and that
boy in the middle, as the mother couldn't 'ardly

bear to part with, not even to let 'im wash 'is face
and 'ands afore 'avin' some supper, as they made
me stop and drink 'is 'ealth in a bowl of punch, as
were made in a cheyney bowl, as 'ad been in the
family for years, and a good many of Mrs. Camplin's
brothers and sisters 'ad been christened in it,
as I don't consider a proper use for a punch-
bowl myself, for I always say, "everythink in
its place, and a place for everythink," as the
sayin' is.

When that young feller were washed and
brushed up a bit, he looked downright 'andsome,
tho' 'is clothes was wore out, and he'd suffered
frightful 'ardships thro' that coral reef, as is a
nasty thing to fall on, as I've see a bit on myself,
and looks for all the world like a putrefied sponge;
but all 'is troubles was over now, and so was 'is
poor dear mother's, not as either 'er or me never
espected 'im to steady down like as he did ever
arter, and in a year or two a-walkin' the 'ospitals
as steady as a rock.

No doubt that coral reef, as is only a rock arter
all, 'ad been a lesson to 'im, and the sea-woyage
done 'im good, for he'd been with one of 'em
captins as is reg'lar martingales, as the sayin' is,
for strickness, and thro' a narrer escape of bein' eat
by them savages, didn't seem to mind the dissectin'
a bit, thro' 'avin' got used to it, for use is second

natur' arter all, as is no doubt why them savages
oats their feller-creeturs iu sandwiches over there.

But as I were a-sayin' to 'is mother the werry
night he turned up alive ag'in, I says, "There's
many a cloudy mornin' as 'ave turned out a fine
day, as the sayin' is, so," I says, "he'll do credit
to you yet, mark my words," as said to me, a-sayin',
"good night," tho' jest on three in the mornin',
"Bless you, dear Mrs. Browu, as were a prophet of
good, and give me 'ope and comfort for the New
Year."

"Ah!" I says, "mum, there's comfort for us
all, if we will but take it, and," I says, "let us 'ope
always, for," I says, "without that we shouldn't
ever care to see another Old Year out nor yet the
New Year in."

VI.

TWELFTH NIGHT.

I DON'T know 'ow it is, but I never did think much of Twelf' Night, nor 'ardly ever know'd it kep' since the time when I lived in service where there was a grand ball in Portlan' Place, and they drawed King and Queen, as was a young lady and gentleman as ad crowns on their 'eads made of gilt paper, and 'im with 'is 'air curled, and a bright blue skilington suit and silver buttons, and a frill as were took ill in the middle of it, and spilte the fun, and 'is own clothes, let alone the carpet, as is frequent the end of them things, as always over-eats theirselves, as don't do with dancin'

I must say it was a werry pretty party tho', with a gallanty show and snap-dragon, as nearly frightened some of them little dears to death, thro' bein' done all in the dark, and the way as they was trod into the carpet, thro' bein' throwed all about the room in the scramble, as some got too many, and some none at all, thro' fear of burnin' their fingers, and 'ad to be reg'lar scraped off the next mornin' with a knife, as were a sticky mess, and for my part I do not 'old with playin' with fire any'ow, as is sure to end bad.

I werry well knows as Twelf' Day did used to be kep' werry grand at the West End, partikler at confectioners, for I well remembers a aunt of my dear mother's, as were 'ead pew-opener at St. Martin's-in-the-Fields, and did used to lay out the Communion reg'lar for parties to receive in black silk, as paid 'arf a guinea, and was registered in the parish books, or else couldn't pass the Trust and Corporation, nor 'old no place under gover'ment, with 'er cap trimmed in white love, as always wore mournin', and did always used to go to spend the evenin' at a large pastrycook's near Cherrin' Cross, where the shop-winders was full of lovely cakes, and lighted up with wax-candles along the counter afore gas were knowed iu shops, and drawed King and Queen with crowds round the place, as did used to play their tricks a-pinnin' parties together by their clothes, as was lookin' iu at the winder, and often led to words, let alone tearin' their things, as ain't no fun, even for Christmas time.

All them things is altered now, tho' in course Twelf' Cakes is to be seen, but nothink like what they did used to be, tho' for my part we never took

no notice on it, escept my dear mother did used to
call it Old Christmas-day, as I've 'eard say they did
used to keep in January, as must 'ave made great
confusion, thro' a-bein' in it so near Pancake-day,
as in gin'ral is Febuary.

But as I was a-sayin' I never kep' it myself no
ways partikler, and never should 'ave thought of
such a thing only thro' that Mrs. Spaldin's impidence,
and not if I was to live a thousan' year, and then die
of old age, you wouldn't ketch me a-doiu' it ag'in,
as were a friendly act, and no more notion of
defraudin' nobody than the babe unborn, as is
what I wouldn't stoop to was it ever so, let alone
bein' found out, as is 'eavy penalties, and so it did
ought to be, as is downright robbery for anyone to
be bankrupt, and then keep back everythink, the
same as Mrs. Everton, as 'ad the brokers in the
'ousc, and to my certing knowledge kep' all the
silver, and walked out of the 'ouse with it, and the
family Bible tied round 'er waist, under 'er shawl,
and two pillers, as looked for all the world like
crinerleens, and so took in the man as were in possession, let alone the things as was sent out of the
'ouse with the things a-goin' to the wash, as I
always set my face ag'in.

So I didn't feel comfortable when Mrs. Spaldin
come in two days afore New Year's Day, a. sayin' as
Spaldin' were in difficulties thro' a-puttin' 'is 'and

to a bill, and she should 'ave the bed took from under 'er.

I couldn't but think of the money as they spent down at Margate the summer afore, when ducks and fowls, with 'ot'ouse grapes, and out in open carriages was 'er daily 'abits, and dressed on the jetty as if she'd been Queen Wictoria a-walkin', as is too much the lady, I know, for to go about in a sky-blue dress a-trailin' behind, with pink silk stockin's, and them sand-boots as she'd 'old that 'igh as show'd they was cotton tops, and a-dancin' like mad at the balls every evenin', for all the world like a single woman all the week, and then of a Saturday when Spaldin' were there, a-settin' as mute as a mouse, as the sayin' is, as is artful behaviour as I can't abear, and a-ridin' out on 'orseback with that young feller, as said he was in the milingtary, and found out as were only a 'airdresser's 'sistant close ag'in the Angel, Islington, and a married man, over forty into the bargin, with 'is 'air dyed, as I always said them whiskers was too glossy to be true.

Well, 'ow I come to listen to 'er, and give the things 'ouse-room, was thro' 'er a-sayin' as 'er own brother 'ad bought in the best of 'er furniture for 'er, and thro' a-knowin' as my fust-floor back was unfurnished begged and prayed for me to give a few things 'ouse-room till she could get a place.

Little did I think as she'd 'ave the impidence to send me a good wan-load in that werry day, as made my passage and stair-carpets like a pig-sty, thro' it bein' a wet evenin' when they was brought in.

So I had 'em all packed away in the back room, and locked the door, and the next mornin', when Mrs. Spaldin' come in, I gives 'er the key.

She says, "Oh, dear, this won't never do. I can't make a ware'ouse of your nice 'ouse, they'll be spilte, as was packed in a 'urry," so she set to work and she undoes everything, and puts 'em about the 'ouse, a-fittin' up the back room like a reg'lar bed-room.

She see me a-starin', and says, "I'm a-goin' to encroach so far, Mrs. Brown, as to ask you to 'ave Georgina's pianer in your back parlour, as 'er godpa give 'er, and she's a-learnin' to play on beautiful."

"Well," I says, "I do not mind a-givin' the pianer 'ouse-room, but can't say as I can 'ave 'er comin' in with music a-playin' all day long."

"Oh," she says, "the dear gal is a-goin' to stop over at 'Omerton along with 'er aunt."

So the pianer come that werry arternoon, and as sure as fate Georgina, along with 'er mother, come in about seven o'clock, as wet as rags, and Mrs. Spaldin' said as she'd been obliged to fetch Georgina from 'Omerton, thro' 'er aunt's eldest bein' took with the small-pox, and, she says, "I know'd as you'd be my friend, Mrs. Brown, and give us a bed for a night."

Well, I must say I was put out thro' a-suspectin' as it was all a trick, for, bless you, that woman 'ad reg'lar fitted up that back fust floor of mine, as if she was settled there for life.

I do think she meant for to stop ever so long, for the next mornin' she come down a-sayin' as Georgina were that feverish as she wouldn't let 'er get up, but would take 'er up a cup of tea and a bit of dry toast.

In course I couldn't say her nay under them circumstances, but I says, "I do 'ope as she'll be all right soon, for I can't ask you to stop any longer than for a day or so, as Brown may be 'ome any time, and would be nicely put out to find as I'd a sick 'ouse."

"Oh," she says, "my hangel gal will niver be in nobody's way; and I'm sure 'er mother 'ave too much sperrit to let 'er stop anywheres as she isn't welcome."

The werry next mornin' I got a letter from Brown, a-sayin' as he couldn't be 'ome for a week, as I kep' dark from that woman, as I did not fancy, and don't believe as there was much the matter with that gal, tho' she did keep 'er room, for often I 'eard 'er a-laughin' like mad along

with 'er mother, when they thought I was gone to
bed.

So when they'd been there three days, and didn't
give no signs of goin', I says to Mrs. Spaldin' as
I could not ask 'er to stop no longer.

She says, " I was just a-goin' to speak to you
about takin' your room and a-payin' for our board."

I says, " When I wants to let lodgin's I shall
put up a bill, thank you, mum; but as I ain't a-goin'
to do no such a thing, I'd rather 'ave my 'ouse to
myself."

She says, " Well, I think as you're right, for it's
a pokey 'ole for a family, and I should 'ave to ask
you to keep a better table if I stopped, as 'ave
never been used to dine off cold meat and a
puddin'."

I says, " I ouly 'opes as you may never 'ave a
worse dinner than a fine bit of cold sirloin aud a
apple puddin' as I made myself, with a thin crust
and a bit of lemon peel, and a clove or two for
flaviour, and 'ad give 'er a 'ot supper two nights
runnin', as is not a thing we 'ave in a gen'ral
way; aud the way as she'd put away her bottled
beer, a-toppin' up with sperrits and water, I did
think was table good enough for any one.

She went on a-sayin', " In my pa's lifetime we
never set down without fish and soup, and 'ad
dessert every day."

"Ah," I says, "you can't eat your cake and have it."

As she said was a unfeelin' remark, and pretended for to wipe 'er eyes, a-sayin' as I'd spoke ag'in 'er pa, as I've 'eard say were a reg'lar old swindler in the corn-chandlerin' line.

I didn't say a word more 'opin' as I'd offended 'er, for that gal of 'ern, as 'ad come down was a-drivin' me mad with "My cottage near the sea," on the pianer, as she played wrong with one finger by the 'our together. At last I couldn't stand it no longer, and says, "You'll escuse me a-speakin', but if you don't shet up that pianer I will, as is enough to drive any one mad, and shall 'ave the neighbours sendin' in."

"Come away, my love," says Mrs. Spaldin', "come to your 'art-broken mother," and out of the room they both goes a-'owlin' and wouldn't come down to tea, and went out jest arter, a-slammin' the front door without a word.

Well, I didn't know what to do to get rid on 'em thro' it's bein' Christmas time when they come, but nearly over, as I would not shet my door on 'em for the world, but 'ad made up my mind as they should walk when Christmas were over at the latest, as it were a few days arter New Year's-day as I'd 'ad them words about the pianer, as she took on so all about.

That werry evenin' I were fetched all of a' urry to see Brown's aunt, as 'ad been took sudden ill, and the doctor said wasn't many 'ours to live; so off I went without leavin' a word for Mrs. Spaldin', as 'ad gone out like that, espectin' to be 'ome afore she were a-bed, and then should give 'er the 'int to go.

I did used to go in werry often to that aunt of Brown's, not as she cared for me nor me for 'er, for that matter, but as she were a-failin' fast, I give 'er a look in. So went off, a-tellin' the gal as I might be late, tho' not certain.

When I got to the old lady's, I see with 'arf a eye as she'd 'ad 'er death-blow, as were in bed and know'd me, and seemed glad to see me, and asked me to stop a bit.

I says, " Yes, I'm in no 'urry partikler," and set by 'er bed-side, as were very dosey, tho' she kep' startin' and lookin' round, and seemed satisfied when she see me, not as I was wanted, leastways didn't think I was, as she 'ad a nuss as 'ad looked arter 'er for years, in the name of Garmin, a werry good creetur, as come into the room jest then.

When I see 'er legs, as was swelled like bolsters, and cold as hice, I says to 'er, " You go and lay down this werry hinstant," as 'ad been up three nights, as will swell the leg, we all know.

She was thankful to do it, and off she went. I

set there alone with that old woman, and was
a-lookin' at 'er thro' the fire a-blazin' up, and
a-thinkin' what a remarkable plain old woman she
were, when I see as 'er eyes was wide open
a-starin' at me.

So I goes up to the bedside, in a low tone a-
askin' 'er if she wanted anythink, quite a-forgettin' she were deaf, and was took a-back when she
spoke out in a laudable woice, and says, " Yes, I
wants to die."

I says, " We must all wait our time, and nobody
didn't ought to wish to die afore their time is
come." I was more a-thinkin' than a-speakin' not
believin' as she could 'ear.

She says, " Do you think that I can stand this
much longer ?"

I says, " It's werry bad no doubt," a-knowin' as
'er asma bothered 'er at nights.

She says, " You needn't talk so loud ; I ain't so
deaf as I can't 'ear you."

So I says, " Oh, indeed ;" and was a-wonderin'
whether she'd been a-pretendin' deafness all them
years, as she was quite capable on, thro' bein' one
of the downiest old parties as ever I met with, and
I've seen a many.

So she says, " I wants to see Sarah."

I says, " So you shall if I 'ave to walk barefoot
to find 'er."

She ketches 'old of my harm and says, "Yes;
I want to see 'er ; I want to tell her 'ow I 'ope my
curse may foller 'er thro' life and death."

I was took aback; I shakes 'er off and I says,
"You wicked old wretch, 'ow dare you say sich a
hawful thing !"

She says, "I 'ates and detests 'er."

So I says, "Go to sleep, do, you're a-ravin',
and say your prayers."

She says, "Get out of my sight; where's that
old fool, Garmin. Why does she leave me 'ere
with you ?"

I says, "Because she must get some rest;" and
I says, "come, that's a dear soul, do try and sleep
a-bit."

She says, "I shall never sleep ag'in ; but," she
says, "I do want to tell that gal of mine 'ow I
'ates 'er."

So I says, "Whyever do you 'ate your own
flesh and blood, as is ag'in natur. What's she
done ?"

She says, "You know."

"Well," I says, "she were wrong, and foolish
to marry ; but that ain't so bad arter all."

She says, "She married the man as 'ad been
courtin' me."

I did think as I should 'ave busted out a-larfin',
but I kep' my feelin's under by sayin', "Well,

I'm sure, you'd a lucky escape, for he was a bad lot."

She says, "Not at all; I could 'ave made 'im a comfortable 'ome, as she never did, and then for 'im to come a-carneyin' me, and borrer'd the werry money as they got married with. Oh, how I should like to serve 'em both out."

Well, the wiolence as she'd been and give way to brought on sich a fit of coughin' as I were obligated to set the winder wide open, and prop 'er up in bed, for to get 'er breath, and thought as I must call Mrs. Garmin, for the old creetur's eyes was a-rollin', as I thought she were stranglin'; but arter a bit she come 'round, and says to me, "I knows I'm dyin', but," she says, "I will see 'er."

"Lor!" I says, "why it's so many year ago, and was no doubt werry aggrawatin';" but I says to 'er, "forgive and forget, for," I says, "I'm sure she's paid dear enough for the life as that butcher-boy led 'er, and then emigrated along with the bar-maid at the 'Flyin' Salmon,' as was always a bold 'ussey."

But, lor, you might as well try and talk to the bed-post as to old Mrs. Bundy, as were 'er name, and 'ad married Bundy 'erself ag'in 'er father's will.

As to Brown, he never would 'ear 'er name, nor foller 'er to the grave, and called 'er a old wretch; but as the seventy pounds were left to me, in course

I took it, and agreed with Brown as we'd give it
to that poor Mrs. Child's, as were Mrs. Bundy's
daughter's name, thro' a-marryin' of the butcher-
boy as was as bandy a young thief as ever got
across a 'orse when I fust knowed 'im, and the way
as he'd gallop down the Bow Road was enough for
to strike terror to the 'art, and rode slap over the
cat's-meat barrer one Monday, as was nothink but
spite, and werry nigh killed Mrs. Shean as did used
to set close ag'in the corner by Tredeager Square,
with 'er little stall winter and summer, and 'owever
she could live at it I can't think, as 'er whole stock
couldn't never 'ave been more than a shillin's worth;
and the strongest peppermint drops as ever I tasted,
as is a fine thing for any one with a weak stomich
as I've knowed give relief instant.

So she was quiet for a bit, and then she says to
me, "You're precious fond of preachin', and I
don't want none of your sermons, but jest ring the
bell for Garmin."

I says, "She's reg'lar wore out, and 'ave gone
to get a little rest; so let me set along with
you."

She says, "I shan't. I'll 'ave Garmin down if
she's dyin'."

"Well, then," I says, "you won't, and that's
flat; for I shan't call 'er, and you may do your
worst."

She tried to get up, as I knowed she couldn't, and she raved at me wiolent.

So I says, " I'm your nearest blood relation's wife, and," I says, "if you don't be quiet, I'll 'ave two doctors 'ere to sign your certifikit as you're mad, and I'll 'ave you took to a mad-'ouse, as is the best place for you."

Them words seemed to quiet 'er, and then she begun a-wimperin', a-sayin' as I was usin' 'er shameful, and when the doctor come she'd order me out of the 'ouse.

I says, " I shall be gone long afore that, so," I says, " you lay still, unless you wants a straight westkut on."

Tho' she were a old wretch as 'ad be'aved bad to every one, I wouldn't 'ave bullied 'er, only that poor Mrs. Garmin were nearly as bad as she were; as I went up to see and found 'er gone off that sound as I wouldn't wake 'er, so stopped with old Mrs. Bundy all night, as slep' pretty well 'erself.

When mornin' come she was in the dead sulks, and didn't even blow poor Garmin up, and never said a word about me to the doctor, as I waited to see and come in full late in the arternoon, and what kep' 'er quiet was thro' bein' afeard as I might let out a few things about 'er as I knowed.

As I thought, the doctor said as Garmin must 'ave rest, or he wouldn't answer for 'er legs; so I said as I'd go 'ome for a few things, a-promisin' as I'd return the last thing.

When I got to my place, as were jest on dusk, you might 'ave knocked me down with a feather; for if I didn't find all the place upset, and lots of things about the room as the gal told me Mrs. Spaldin' 'ad brought in three cabs, and my best tea-things out; and if Mrs. Spaldin' didn't say, dressed out ever so fine and all smiles, "Oh, dear Mrs. Brown, I'm so glad to see you, for I've asked one or two friends in to tea, as it's my dear gal's birthday and Twelfth Night, you know, and I was so wexed at your not bein' at home."

"Well," I says, "you're a cool 'and, certingly," but didn't say no more, as she'd asked Mrs. Toulmin and Mrs. Archbut, as come in jest then, thro' bein' friends of mine, as I wouldn't 'ave insulted a-shettin' my door in their face, for the world.

I certingly never were more surprised than when I see the supper as that woman 'ad ordered in, as were laid out in the back parlour, with cold chicken and 'am and a pigeon-pie from the pastry-cook's, along with jellies and tarts, and all manner.

Mrs. Spaldin' says, "Don't it look pretty; you 'ardly knows your own 'ome."

I says, "I certingly don't, and wants to know who's to pay for it all?"

She says, "I 'opes I'm too much the lady to

order things as I can't pay," but she says, "that's a good soul, do make yourself agreeable for once in a way, for," she says, "I espects my brother and a friend as is rollin' in riches."

Well, for Mrs. Archbut's sake, I thought I'd stop a bit afore goin' back to Brown's aunt, so put on my cap and gownd and went down to take tea with them.

"Ah," says Mrs. Spaldin', "now we're all right," and were that attentive to me, a-makin' that gal and me toast and tea-cakes, as I must say I did relish, thro' 'avin 'ad nothink 'ardly for dinner at Mrs. Bundy's, as always 'arf starved Garmin and the gal as she kep'.

Mrs. Spaldin' she kep' a-goin' on about my enjoyin' my tea, and sayin', "That's right. Ah, I wish as you'd let me order things for you always, as reg'lar enjoys good livin', I knows."

I didn't make no remark, and as soon as tea were over, that Nancy Spaldin' tried for to play on the pianer, as was a beastly row, and then a young friend of 'ern named Julia Biles played, as wasn't much better; and as to 'er young man as tried to sing "Hever of thee," cats was concerts to 'im; partikler when she would chime in along with Nancy Spaldin', a-'clpin' 'im thro' with it, as she said.

Mrs. Spaldin' said as we'd 'ave supper at nine,

as 'er brother 'ad promised faithful to be with 'er by that time.

So we 'ad a game at all fours, not as I could foller it, for the distractin' row as them young people kep' a-kickin' up at that pianer, I was glad when Mrs. Spaldin's brother come in to stop it.

Certingly that Mr. Rufford, as was 'er brother's name, might 'ave been rollin' in riches, for where there's muck there's money, as the sayin' is; but he looked a deal more like rollin' in the mud; and as to the man as was with 'im, as he called 'is friend Giffin, he was beastly dirty, and the wuss for liquor.

I couldn't a-bear the look of either on 'em, as made the place smell of rum like pison; and as to their manners, no costers wouldn't 'ave forgot theirselves, for if they didn't make that free with Mrs. Spaldin', and as to Nancy, that feller Giffin made that free with 'er as to make me say to 'er mother on the quiet, as I didn't consider it proper goin's on.

"Law!" she says, "what a old frump you are to be sure; why he's come a-courtin' 'er."

"What," I says, "why he must be near fifty, and 'er not seventeen."

She says, "What of that, as is often done in the fust families, as Queen Wictoria's daughters ain't settled much older."

" Now," I says, " Mrs. Spaldin, do you mean to
say as you'd let that dirty, 'arf-drunken old beast
marry your child, for a child she is ?"

She says, " She will 'ave 'im whether I like it
or no."

I says, " 'Ow long 'ave she knowed 'im ?"

" Oh," she says, " ever so long."

I didn't say nothink, a-knowin' she were a-
tellin' false'oods by 'er way, and as we'd been a-
lookin' to the supper in the back-room, as were
now ready, Mrs. Spaldin' she opens the foldin'-doors
and asks 'em all in, jest as if it 'ad been 'er 'ouse
and me a mere syphon to be made use on.

Well, I didn't at all relish my supper, thro' the
way as them men went on, and that feller Rufford
a-encouragin' that Giffin in 'is free ways, and as to
that gal Nancy, she were downright bare-faced, a-
puttin' tartlets in 'is mouth, and a-larfin' and goin'
on so as I could see as both Mrs. Archbut and Mrs.
Tonlmin was quite a-blushin' for 'er, and would 'ave
said somethink, but for their attention bein' took
off with their suppers, as they certingly did enjoy.

When supper were over, there was punch and
sperrits and water, as Mrs. Spaldin' 'ad laid in, and
then Rufford sang a werry wulgar sort of song
about parties a-courtin' under a umbreller.

Then old Giffin made a speech, that thick as I
couldn't 'ardly 'ear a word as he said, and then if

he didn't take and kiss Nancy and 'er mother under the missletoe, as Mrs. Spaldin' 'ad 'ung up no doubt for the purpose under the gas chandleer, and then if he didn't say as he'd kiss the lot.

I says, "Stand back, if you please, and don't you make that free a-kissin' parties as don't 'ardly know you. Keep to them as does and likes it."

"Why," he says, "I knows you almost as well as I knows them, for I never set eyes on 'em afore yesterday, as they was brought to my place."

I says, "'Ow can that be, when you've been a-courtin' that young gal ever so long?"

He bust out a-larfin' that wiolent, with 'is mouthful, as made 'im jump up for to get 'is breath, and, in settin' down, he missed his chair, and come flop ou the floor, enough to bring the 'ouse down.

I says to that Rufford, "'Elp 'im up;" but jest then that Giffin gave a clutch at me, and dragged me down too. I seized old of Mrs. Spaldin', as caught by the table, and pulled everythink off, includin' my cap and 'air, as come off in the confusion.

The row as we made brought up the gal and a strange man, as I see a-glarin' round at everybody, as says, "Pretty ways for them to go on as 'ave got the brokers in."

I jumps up, a-puttin' my cap and 'air on in a

'urry, and says, "Mrs. Spaldin', there must be a
stop put to this, so jest tell your friends to go ;"
and I says to the strange man, " Whatever business
'ave you 'ere ?"

He says, " Business !   I'll soon let you know,
and so will the Sheriff."

I says to the gal, " When did you let 'im in ?"

She says, " More than a-'our ago, and he's
been settin' in the kitchen."

I says, " Why didn't you tell me ?"

" 'Cos," she says, " that woman said as she would
see 'im when he come in, told me not to interfere, but 'ave now found out as he's the brokers."

I thought I should 'ave died when that feller
went on to say as it were so, and he'd took possession.

Then I says, " Whatever for ?   Get out o' my
'ouse, as you ain't no right to be 'ere with no
possession."

He says, " Yes I have, for you've been a-
'arbourin' goods 'as have been removed from this
woman's 'ouse, where I was in possession, as is
felony.   This ten days, along with my mate, I've
watched the cab as brought the things to this 'ouse."

Mrs. Spaldin', she set on the sofy a-coverin' 'er
face with 'er 'ands, Nancy were a-sobbin', Old
Giffin a-settin' lookin' foolish, and Rufford were
'on the floor speechless.

That young man as were keepin' compauy with
Julia Biles said as she shouldn't stay in such a den
no longer, and off they went.

Mrs. Archbut she spoke up for me to that
broker's man, thro' bein' wife to my landlord, and
so did Mr. Toulmin as know'd me to be respectable, and certingly it's a providence they was both
there at 'and to 'elp me.

So I says to Mrs. Spaldin', "'Ow dare you make
my place a leavin'-shop, as ain't no better than
receivin' stolen goods as is transportation; and,
you false 'ooman, you told me your brother 'ad
bought it all in."

She didn't say nothink, but that Old Giffin says,
"'im buyin' anythink in! 'im as 'aven't got a mag to
bless 'imself with, as 'ave been borrerin' of me—
robbin' me, I may say."

"Who's been a-robbin' you?" says Rufford.

"Why, you 'ave, with your rich sister and 'er
lovely gal as you brought me to supper with; but
now I've found you out as 'ave 'ticed me into this
old waggerbone's place, as looks more like a thief
than a 'orse 'erself."

I couldn't stand that, so I says, "Sarah Ann,
open the front door;" and I says to them two
fellers, "Now, you walk, both on you; step it,
this werry instant. And you too," I says to Mrs.
Spaldin'.

Says that Giffin, "I'll give you all in charge for 'ocussin' me."

I calls out to Sarah Ann, as were at the door 'oldin' it open for 'em to go, " If you see a perliceman jest 'ave 'im in," as come up at that werry moment, and walks into the parlour.

I says to 'im, " I want all these men turned out, as is my own 'ouse, and they are 'ere ag'in my will."

That broker's man begun a-sayin' as he wouldn't leave, as 'ad lawful right to be there; but that 'ere Rufford he sloped, as the sayin' is, and that 'ere Giffin follered 'im.

I says to Sarah Ann, "Jest step over and ask Mr. Camplin if he'll come 'ere for a minit, likewise Mr. Archbut," as lived oppersite, and was espected 'ome late, I knowed, for she told me he'd promised to fetch 'is good lady 'ome.

They both come over, and on 'earin' my tale, and me a-promisin' as nothink shouldn't leave the 'ouse till they was fetched away in the mornin', that broker's man went away quite civil with a glass of sperrits and water.

As to Mrs. Spaldin', I says to 'er, " I wouldn't turn a dog out, thro' bein' a fieldmale myself at this 'our, so you may stay till the mornin', but you don't stop 'ere, as may go to your own room ; but off you are the fust thing, and never dare show

your deceitful face to me ag'in, and as to your
things, off they goes to them as 'ave a right to
'em."

It's lucky as Sarah Ann 'ad 'eard the deceitful
cat say as the things 'ad been bought in for 'er, or
she'd 'ave swore as I were in the swindle; not as
she tried to brazen it out then, but went upstairs
with 'er gal a-blubberin' like a wail, as the
sayin' is.

When the 'ouse were cleared, Mr. Camplin and
Mr. Archbut set down with us for a bit; and give
me good adwice with Mrs. Archbut and Mrs. Toulmin, not as they could say much, thro' that woman
'avin' took them in with borrered money, not as
they know'd it wasn't my party, for she'd come and
told 'em as it were my wishes as they should come
thro' bein' jest a few friends, and then to say as
that gal's godpa 'ad give 'er the twelfthcake, as
were only a five-shillin' one, as she'd bought and
not paid for, ag'in Mile End Gate.

We set there till past twelve, for it is downright wonderful 'ow time does fly in pleasant company, with jest a-'avin' of a bit of a chat, with a
a glass of punch or so, all went 'ome on the stroke
of one.

As in course I couldn't leave the 'ouse no
more that night, with that woman in it, I didn't
mind, and 'ad sent the gal in a cab to Mrs.

Bundy's, for to say as 'ow I couldn't come back.

She wasn't long gone, and come in a-sayin' as the old lady were werry quiet, and they could manage thro' Mrs. Garmin's sister 'avin' looked in ; so I locks up the 'ouse, and took the keys of the doors up to bed with me, for fear of that woman a-playin' any tricks, and glad I was to think, when I'd got to bed, as all were over so well.

I was up and down the fust thing next mornin', and there was Mrs. Spaldin' and 'er gal with their bonnets on, all ready to start, as begged and prayed as I'd let 'er take a few things away in a cab

" No," I says, " nothink but your things for a change, and I told Sarah Ann to make 'em some tea, but wouldn't set down with 'em, nor yet shake 'ands with 'er at partin', as might 'ave transported me with their wile swindlin' ways, as I ound out arterwards was a old trick of 'ers, and that feller no more 'er brother than me, and as to Spaldin' it were a false name, as 'ad been in prison twice for embezzlin', as means stealin' in plain English; and what makes me so mad is, as I shouldn't never 'ave knowed 'er at all only thro' a-comin' for the character of a servant, and then kep' it up thro' a-pretendin' to 'ave took sich a fancy to me, as only shows as we didn't ever ought to give in to no flatterers.

About ten, them brokers come for the goods, and glad I was when they was all cleared out, and about twelve o'clock if the pastrycook's boy didn't come with sich a bill, to fetch away 'is dishes and things as I 'ad to pay, and the poulterer, and fruiterer as well, for that woman was a downright swindler all over the place.

I really did feel that reg'lar upset as I could not go out that day as were werry cold and drizzly, and my 'ead terrible bad, so required nussin' myself, and that kind soul, Mrs. Archbut, come and set with me to a early cup of tea, so it wasn't till the next day, thro' a-feelin' myself better, as I went to Mrs. Bundy, as 'ad rallied, and didn't die for more than six months arter that, and see poor old Garmin in the grave afore 'er ; but she never spoke no more about seein' 'er daughter, as were that rheumatic, as move she couldn't, if she'd wanted to, as run in the family by the father's side.

When Brown come 'ome, and I told 'im all about Mrs. Spaldin's little caper, and he says, " It's my opinion as you'll end your days either in a jail for breakin' of the laws, or else a mad'ouse, as I must put you in for fear as you should do yourself a injury."

" Well," I says, " Brown, I only did it neighbourly like, and never could 'ave believed in such double-faced 'ippocripsy ; but," I says, " never no

more in this world will I take in any one's goods
nor chapels either."

I'd 'ad my lessons, as the sayin' is, and that's
why I think it is as I don't care about Twelf'
Night so much, tho' in course it's Christmas all the
same, and some parties takes down the 'olly arter
that, tho' some keeps it up to Candlemas, as is
when the days is a-gettin' out ag'in.

Not but what Twelf' Night is a pretty sight as
is kep' up by the Lady Maress with a juvenile ball,
as is certingly a treat for the young folks, and good
for trade, for, as I were a-sayin' to Miss Masklin,
do away with all them days, and things like that,
and what becomes of your trades, partikler 'air-
dressers and pastrycooks, as we can't do without,
unless we was all to go back to live in caves with
a blanket skewered round us, the same as they did
used to when Julius Cæsar were king, as must 'ave
been rough times, a-livin' on acorns, as I never
will believe myself can be nourishin', as is as bitter
as 'orse chesnuts, and 'ard as nails, as it's well
known even King George couldn't get the bul-
locks to eat, as 'ad too much sense, a-knowin' it
would spile their beef, tho' I 'ave 'eard say as
pigs makes werry nice pork with acorns; but I
says all seasons 'as their dishes, as all comes in turn,
as is wisely ordered, no doubt, tho' in course some
will over-eat theirselves all the year round, as is

nasty greed to encourage in young people, thro'
'avin' often a eye as is bigger than their stomichs,
as the sayin' is, and did ought to be checked by
their elders a-settin' them a good esample.   Not as
they will always be trained up in the way as they
should go, as the sayin' is.

F. BENTLEY AND CO., PRINTERS, SHOE LANE, LONDON.

CHRISTMAS PRESENTS AND NEW YEAR'S GIFTS.

The season having arrived, wherein, by exchange of presents, we confirm the stability of friendship, all classes of the community who would successfully cultivate regard by acceptable offerings, will avail themselves of ROWLANDS' Toilet Articles, the MACASSAR OIL, KALYDOR, and ODONTO, each of infallible attributes.

A few words on their inestimable qualities may not inappropriately follow.

Of the numerous compounds constantly announced for promoting the growth or reproduction of the human Hair, few survive, even in name, beyond a very limited period, whilst ROWLANDS' MACASSAR OIL, with a reputation already unparalleled, is still on the increase in public estimation. Among the chief virtues incident to the use of Rowlands' Macassar Oil (in reference to ladies' hair) may he reckoned its enduring properties in preserving the coiffure in pristine decorative beauty through the heat of the hall room, or the locomotion of the promenade. Price 3s. 6d., 7s., 10s. 6d., and 21s. per bottle.

FOR THE SKIN AND COMPLEXION

ROWLANDS' KALYDOR is unequalled for its rare and inestimable qualities. The radiant bloom it imparts to the cheek, the softness and delicacy which it induces of the hands and arms, its capability of soothing irritations and removing cutaneous defects, discolourations, and all unsightly appearances, render it indispensable to every Toilet. Price 4s. 6d. and 8s. 6d. per bottle.

FOR THE TEETH,

ROWLANDS' ODONTO, a white powder, compounded of the choicest and most recherché ingredients of the oriental herbal, is of inestimable value in preserving and beautifying the teeth, strengthening the gums, and in giving a pleasing fragrance to the breath. Price 2s. 9d. per box. Sold by all Chemists and Perfumers.

THE BIRKBECK

Is the ONLY Building Society whose Income exceeds ONE AND A HALF MILLION.

HOW TO PURCHASE A HOUSE FOR TWO GUINEAS PER MONTH,
WITH IMMEDIATE POSSESSION AND NO RENT TO PAY.
Apply at the Office of the BIRKBECK BUILDING SOCIETY,
London Mechanics' Institution, 29, Southampton Buildings, Chancery Lane.

HOW TO PURCHASE A PLOT OF LAND
For Five Shillings per Month,
WITH IMMEDIATE POSSESSION,
Either for Building or Gardening Purposes.
Apply at the Office of the BIRKBECK FREEHOLD LAND SOCIETY,
London Mechanics' Institution, 29, Southampton Buildings, Chancery Lane.

HOW TO INVEST YOUR MONEY WITH SAFETY
AT £5 PER CENT. INTEREST.
App'y at the Office of the BIRKBECK DEPOSIT BANK.
All sums under £50 repayable upon demand.
Current Accounts opened similar to ordinary Bankers. Cheque Books supplied.
Office hours from 11 till 5 daily, on Saturdays from 11 till 2, and on Monday evenings from 7 till 9.

A small Pamphlet, containing full particulars, may be obtained Gratis, or sent Post-free, on application to
FRANCIS RAVENSCROFT, MANAGER.

GEORGE ROUTLEDGE & SONS'
NEW BOOKS FOR CHRISTMAS.

BEAUTIFUL WOMEN. 16 Large Photographs of the finest Female Portraits, by Sir JOSHUA REYNOLDS, GAINSBOROUGH, Sir EDWIN LANDSEER, NEWTON, and SIR THOMAS LAWRENCE, with Descriptive Letterpress by one of our best Art Critics. Large 4to, cloth, gilt edges, 42s.

A DIARY IN THE EAST WITH THE PRINCE AND Princess of Wales. By W. H. RUSSELL, LL.D., with numerous Illustrations (Dedicated by Special Permission to H.R.H. the Princess of Wales). Demy 8vo, cloth, 21s.

BARRINGTON'S PERSONAL SKETCHES OF HIS OWN TIMES. 2 vols., demy 8vo, cloth, 18s.

JORROCKS'S JAUNTS AND JOLLITIES. With 16 Pages of Coloured Plates. Demy 8vo, cloth, 21s.

THE CHILD'S PICTURE BOOK OF WILD AND DO- MESTIC ANIMALS, with Full-page Coloured Pictures by Kronheim. Large oblong, cloth, 10s. 6d.

ROUTLEDGE'S EVERY BOY'S ANNUAL FOR 1870. Edited by EDMUND ROUTLEDGE. With Coloured Plates by Kronheim, and many Illustrations. Demy 8vo, cloth, gilt edges, 6s.

THE PRINCE OF THE HOUSE OF DAVID. With 12 Page Illustrations. Post 8vo, cloth, gilt edges, 5s.

THE THRONE OF DAVID. With 12 Page Illustrations. Post 8vo, cloth, gilt edges, 5s.

THE PILLAR OF FIRE. With 12 Page Illustrations. Post 8vo, cloth, gilt edges, 5s.

FROM LIVERPOOL TO ST. LOUIS. By the Rev. New-MAN HALL, LL.B. Crown 8vo, cloth, 5s.

OURSELVES: ESSAYS ON WOMEN. By E. Lynn LINTON. Crown 8vo, cloth, 5s.

OUR NURSE'S PICTURE BOOK: containing "Tom Thumb," "Babes in the Wood," "Jack and the Bean Stalk," and "Puss in Boots." Large 4to, cloth, 5s.

DORA AND HER PAPA: A New Story for Girls. By the Author of "Lilian's Golden Hours." With Illustrations. Post 8vo, cloth, 5s.

TALES UPON TEXTS. By the Rev. H. C. Adams, M.A. With Illustrations. Post 8vo, cloth, 5s.

THE ILLUSTRATED GIRLS' OWN TREASURY, em-bracing all Pursuits suitable for Young Ladies. With many Illustrations. Post 8vo, cloth, 5s.

CHARACTERISTICS OF WOMEN. By Mrs. Jameson. Post 8vo, cloth, 5s.

DS AND FLOWERS. A New Coloured Book for Children. (Uniform with "Schnick Schnack.") Small 4to, cloth, 5s.

THE GREAT BATTLES OF THE BRITISH ARMY, including the War in Abyssinia. With Coloured Illustrations. Post 8vo, cloth, 5s.

RIDICULOUS RHYMES. Drawn by H. S. Marks. Printed in Colours by Vincent Brooks. 4to. Fancy cover, 6s.

THE CHILD'S PICTURE BOOK OF DOMESTIC ANIMALS. With 12 large Coloured Plates by Kronheim. Large oblong, boards, 5s.

EXTRAORDINARY MEN AND WOMEN. In 1 Vol., crown 8vo, cloth, 5s.

GRISET'S GROTESQUES. With Rhymes by Tom Hood. Fancy boards, 3s. 6d.

TOM DUNSTONE'S TROUBLES: A Book for Boys. By Mrs. Eiloart. With Illustrations. Fcap. 8vo, cloth, 3s. 6d.

FRED AND THE GORILLAS. By Thomas Miller. With Illustrations. Fcap. 8vo, cloth, 3s. 6d.

BUNYAN'S PILGRIM'S PROGRESS. In Words of One Syllable. By Mary Godolphin. With Coloured Plates. Cloth, 3s. 6d.

THE YOUNG MAROONERS. By the Rev. R. Goulding. With Illustrations. Fcap. 8vo, cloth, 3s. 6d.

THE ADVENTURES OF ROBIN HOOD. With Illustrations. Fcap. 8vo, cloth, 3s. 6d.

ROUTLEDGE'S 3s. 6d. POETS. New Volumes:—
1. Chaucer. | 2. Willis.

ROUTLEDGE'S 3s. 6d. REWARDS. New Volumes. Fcap. 8vo, cloth, with Illustrations, gilt edges, 3s. 6d.
1. The Seven Wonders of the World. | 2. Romance of Adventure.

ONE BY ONE: A Child's Book of Tales and Fables. With 50 Illustrations by Oscar Pletsch and Others. Cloth, gilt edges, 3s. 6d.

RHYME AND REASON: A Picture Book of Verses for Little Folks. With 50 Illustrations by Wolf and Others. Cloth, gilt edges, 3s. 6d.

THE GOLDEN HARP: Hymns, Rhymes, and Songs for the Young. With 50 Illustrations. 4to, cloth, 3s. 6d.

THE LIFE OE NAPOLEON. With Plates by John Gilbert. Fcap. 8vo, cloth, 2s. 6d.

ANECDOTES OF DOGS. By the Rev. Charles Williams, M.A. Illustrated. Fcap. 8vo, cloth, 2s.

GEORGE ROUTLEDGE & SONS,

LONDON AND NEW YORK.

ARTHUR SKETCHLEY'S WORKS.

Price ONE SHILLING Each.

Uniform with " Mrs. Brown's Christmas Box."

Mrs. Brown in London.

Mrs. Brown at the Seaside.

Mrs. Brown up the Nile.

Mrs. Brown in the Highlands.

Mrs. Brown's Visits to Paris.

Miss Tomkins's Intended.

LONDON:

G. ROUTLEDGE & SONS, THE BROADWAY, LUDGATE.

Routledge's Cheap Literature (continued).

Price 2s. each. (Postage 4d.

184 Forest Life in Norway and Sweden *Newland.*	246 Sporting in both Hemispheres *D'Ewes.*
189 Marvels of Science *Fullom.*	254 Horses and Hounds *Scrutator.*
195 Eminent Men and Popular Books *Reprinted from the " Times."*	256 Life in China *Milne.*
	273 Life of Julius Cæsar
230 Biography and Criticism. *Reprinted from the " Times."*	*Archdeacon Williams.*
	277 A Cruise upon Wheels *C. A. Collins.*

ROUTLEDGE'S SIXPENNY NOVELS.

COOPER.	COOPER.	VARIOUS.
1 Waterwitch	11 Two Admirals	A. Ward, His Book
2 Pathfinder	12 Miles Walingford	—— Among the
3 Deerslayer	13 Pioneers	Mormons
4 Mohicans	14 Wyandotte	Nasby Papers
5 Pilot	15 Lionel Lincoln	Major Jack Downing
6 Prairie	16 Afloat and Ashore	Biglow Papers
7 Eve Evingham	17 Bravo	Orpheus C. Kerr
8 Spy	18 Sea Lions	Robinson Crusoe
9 Red Rover	1' The Headsman	Uncle Tom's Cabin
10 Homeward Bound	20 Precaution	Colleen Bawn

BEADLE'S LIBRARY.

1 Seth Jones	25 Oonomoo, the	51 The Silver Bugle
2 Alice Wilde	Huron	52 Pomfret's Ward
3 Frontier Angel	26 The Gold Hunters	53 Quindaro
4 Malaeska	27 The Two Guards	54 Rival Scouts.
5 Uncle Ezekiel	28 Single Eye, the	55 Trapper's Pass
6 Massasoit's	Indians' Terror	56 The Hermit
Daughter	29 Mabel Meredith	57 Oronoco Chief
7 Bill Biddon, Trap-	30 Ahmo's Plot	58 On the Plains
per	31 The Scout	59 The Scout's Prize
8 Backwood's Bride	32 The King's Man	60 Red Plume
9 Natt Todd	33 Kent, the Ranger	61 Three Hunters
10 Myra, the Child of	34 The Peon Prince	62 The Secret Shot
Adoption	35 Irona	63 PrisoneroftheMill
11 The Golden Belt	36 Laughing Eyes	64 Black Hollow
12 Sybil Chase	37 Mahaska, the	65 Seminole Chief
13 Monowano, the	Indian Queen	66 On the Deep
Shawnee Spy	38 Slave Sculptor	67 Captain Molly
14 Brethren of Coast	39 Myrtle	68 Star Eyes
15 King Barnaby	40 Indian Jim	69 The Twin Scouts
16 The Forest Spy	41 Wrecker's Prize	70 The Mad Skipper
1' The Far West	42 The Brigantine	71 Little Mocassin
18 Riflemen of Miami	43 The Indian Queen	72 Doomed Hunter
19 Alicia Newcombs	44 Moose Hunter	73 Eph Peters
20 Hunter's Cabin	45 The Cave Child	74 The Fugitives
21 The Block House	46 The Lost Trail	75 BigFoot,theGuide
22 The Allens	47 Wreck of Albion	76 Ruth Harland
23 Esther; or the	48 Joe Davis's Client	77 Karaibo
Oregon Trail	49 Cuban Heiress	78 TheShawnee'sFoe
24 Ruth Margerie	50 Hunter's Escape	79 The Creole Sisters

ROUTLEDGE'S CHEAP COOKERY BOOKS.

Francatelli's Cookery. 6d.	One Thousand Hints for the Table. 1s.
Soyer's Cookery for the People. 1s.	Mrs. Rundell's Domestic Cookery. 2s.
Mrs. Rundell's Domestic Cookery. 1s.	The British Cookery Book. 3s. 6d.

———o———

LONDON : GEORGE ROUTLEDGE AND SONS.